The author would like to dedicate this book to the close friends who supported him when suffering severe health problems, the doctors and nurses of the Freeman Hospital and the donor (whoever he is) who literally put the heart into this book. Also his daughters and, as always, his darling wife, Kathleen.

R L Pape

BLUEBIRDS IN THE MOONLIGHT

AUSTIN MACAULEY PUBLISHERS™

LONDON • CAMBRIDGE • NEW YORK • SHARJAH

A CIP catalogue record for this title is available from the British Library.

ISBN 9781528990622 (Paperback)
ISBN 9781528990639 (ePub e-book)

www.austinmacauley.com

First Published (2020)
Austin Macauley Publishers Ltd
25 Canada Square
Canary Wharf
London
E14 5LQ

Synopsis

Ever wondered about the people you know, or whether you know them at all? This novel concentrates on that premise. What shapes men and women? What affect have their experiences had on them? What makes them the people they are? This novel spans sixty years from pre-Second World War Oxford to the turn of the millennium. It begins in a local pub where old friends have met each Tuesday and Thursday for almost forty years and provides a link to the main characters whose lives are intertwined.

This novel begins with their current lives as a counterpoint to the people they were, beginning with a young Duncan and Alex who meet at university in Oxford. It follows Duncan through the North African campaigns to Italy where he is injured at Lauro. It's also where he meets his future wife who has her own troubled background.

Fred's background is different. In the forgotten army, in Burma, he was part of the Chindits fighting behind enemy lines, where he was brutalised and at Imphal, where he was traumatised.

Alex witnesses the debacle at Dunkirk. The experience leads to his recruitment to SOE F Section in Baker Street.

Finally, we come to Bob who is determined to escape the colliery village where he was born and marries Joan, a fellow traveller. Together, they are the bright young sixties couple who are befriended by the older group as they all settle in the new city suburbs developing at that time.

The story concludes with Duncan's death and how it has affected them all.

Bluebirds in the Moonlight is a song by Mildred Bailey; the forgotten lady of jazz, that provides a link throughout the story.

Chapter One

Where Bob grew up, it seemed men and women lived separate lives; men worked whilst women stayed at home to look after the house and children. If men thought they ruled the roost, they were mistaken when it came to the home. The home was the reserve of the women and men spent little time there, spending leisure hours during the day on allotments or playing sport; football for the younger men and bowls for the older ones together with dog and pigeon racing. On an evening, it was the clubs and pubs. Men were men then, they didn't care what they looked like and assumed their wives didn't care what they looked like either. Not that they were in for much to notice what their wives thought. When single girls were pursued vigorously, flattered outrageously until marriage vows were taken, accompanied until first child arrived then ignored as you went to the pub. At least that was what it looked like.

But the pub did rule supreme. There were no mobile phones and even if you had a phone at home, you didn't use it. That was for emergencies and stood with its wooden box next to it for coins when the neighbours had an emergency. If you wanted to talk to someone, you went to their local; every man had a local and that's where you found him. Now only the older men have a local, those over forty, which they drink in between the hours of seven and nine twice during the week and on Sunday afternoons in December. The myth of the local continues, but only in the shared memory and sense of nostalgia.

Today is Tuesday and Bob claims his seat. It's his seat every Tuesday and Thursday and he'll give a good scowl to anyone who tries to take it. But they never do; if someone has their own table, it means that it's a proper pub full of locals. And it is full, full of the Tuesday crowd, sitting at their own tables with the same people they sit with every week. Bob's on the right by the bar, Alex has his back the wall and Fred sits tightly on the left in the corner. They never think to change; each has developed his own comfort and is content.

To the casual observer, Fred and Alex are exactly the same as Bob; it's as if their different pasts have led by diverse routes to a common present. In Fred's case, from a comfortable childhood in the professional middle classes to the present via university, the army, the optimistic fifties and melting pot of the sixties. His family always had a penchant for mixing, however, as comfortable in the snug as on the golf course. It gives him a feeling of belonging, of being of the common man and quintessentially English. This means there is no class, just those who are better than others. This isn't to be ashamed of and can't be changed; it's just one of the unfortunate things in life that has to be accepted. And if you accepted it then it meant that you had to control it so forget your liberal tendencies and look to the realities of life. In Fred's opinion, Margaret had it right and he still mourns the day she left office.

Bob also mourns Margaret and thinks that people have to be controlled. When he was growing up, everyone lived in the same village and worked down the colliery. But this didn't mean that everyone was equal, only that some deserved better and were born in the wrong circumstances. His mother went to church, his father went to the club and both looked down their noses at the men in the spit and sawdust pubs who drank their wages whilst their children went barefoot. Bob can't actually remember any child going barefoot but it must have happened as it was the measure of drunkenness and poverty.

In their isolation from other villages and within the narrow confinement of their own streets, they operated the most regimented of societies. The men's jobs dictated which street they lived in, which club they drank in, who they drank with and who their wives and children were friends with. Courting had to be done strictly within these bounds. Bob remembers Edna who he'd desperately wanted and who had turned into the slut his mother had predicted. He also remembers Doreen who'd wanted him but wasn't right. She was still nice but that just proves she was born to the wrong parents. He feels no regrets. These things couldn't happen now and that reassures him.

"Good evening. And, how are you?" Fred's greeting to Bob is the same as he gives every Tuesday and Thursday and every Sunday lunch time in December. It hasn't altered in thirty years and is also given to Alex and anyone else when, on the odd occasion, they join them. Alex merely looks up and smiles, as he does when either Fred or Bob have the floor, which is most of the time.

"As well as can be expected." The answer is also the same as he gives every Tuesday and Thursday and every Sunday lunch time in December. Not that he's ill and he hardly missed a day's work prior to retirement. The slight aches and pains he now suffers, he puts down to hard-earned old age. And if he's earned them then he's entitled to moan about them. Besides, the statement leads to the next ritual part of the conversation.

"I see old Duncan isn't very well." This week, it's Duncan. The name is flexible but the comments are always the same.

"Aye, another one. We're getting old. That's it. Mind you, Duncan was a bit of a bugger when he was younger." Everyone was a bit of a bugger when they were younger. Or maybe it had to do with being young. However, in this case it's true; Duncan was a bit of a bugger. It would be funny if Fred knew how much and realised his wife could probably tell him.

"Still, we soldier on." Fred truly does soldier on like the old soldier he is. Being a soldier was probably the happiest time of his life. In the army, everything was clear, there was an order to things, decisions weren't necessary, everything was black and white and therefore, you knew you were right. And you could be one of the lads but at the same time, a top soldier and therefore, something better. That was why he'd refused a commission and remained a sergeant. He could be one of the lads but better. And he didn't have to set too much of an example. Because in his own way he'd been a bit of a bugger himself.

True soldiering had passed Bob. Whereas Fred and Alex had fought in the war Bob had been called for National Service in the fifties and had never left the British shore. Bob didn't wish to recollect the dreary days stationed near dreary cities, with no money and less hope of finding a girl and having fun. Fred and Alex could talk; although Alex never does.

Alex is sitting listening to the ritual exchange. He's a good listener is Alex. Although maybe he isn't. A good listener is somebody who is sought out when people have a problem, a stooge to open up to, a friend to provide sympathy, a therapist for problems. Alex merely listens. Although it must be said, he listens well and is so unobtrusive people have been known to forget he's there. That's his skill, to be able to join company but be practically invisible, to be part of a crowd whilst being on his own. An outgoing introvert.

Bob and Fred have known him years but don't really know him at all. Alex isn't from the collieries; Bob and Fred know that. He's not really a townie, like Fred, neither. His roots, like his accent, are none descript. This doesn't really matter because Bob and Fred have known him so long that he has history with them even without his early years. The strange thing is, however, that they've never thought about his roots. He can talk intimately about the past without ever leaving the general, use it as a link to his opinions without evoking personal experience. And as his opinions rarely differ from the others, they don't provoke further investigation. But even where they differ, they have been hidden by silence.

"You were in the army with Duncan, weren't you?" Bob knows that the two were contemporaries and have often shared memories over a drink.

"No, not really," Fred replies carefully. It's the careful reply that the observant would recognise as the cue for extensive memories. At one time, these memories had to be prised out of him but now whilst given, at least seemingly, reluctantly they are more readily forthcoming. He actually believes that he is less reticent these days because time has healed wounds and the stories need telling. In reality, he is aware that he has less time left and that he can't afford to resist too forcefully.

"No, Duncan was in North Africa and Italy before D Day whilst I was in Burma before. Bad times Bob, we lost one in three, and did I tell you that. One in three." He has told him that, on several occasions, but it doesn't lose any of its potency with the telling. Fred does bear the scars of his war. Horrors that made him hard at the time, intractable on his return and came as dreams which woke him sweating for years, awakenings which his wife had to calm but which were never acknowledged later. Fears that should have brought more closeness but which ultimately led to greater distance. Fears that meant they could no longer sleep together. But that's not widely known. In fact, it's hardly known at all. Although Duncan knows. But he isn't going to tell.

"It was bad, wasn't it, Alex?" Alex merely nods his head and Fred, happy with the confirmation continues with his story. "But then again we had some laughs. Did I tell you about when we used to go out on a weekend, when we were first demobbed? That's when I first really met Duncan. There were about six of us, all out of the army, and we used to go to this pub in the city on a weekend. Of course, women couldn't really get in pubs in those days so we used to have about five pints then run like hell up the bank to the hall at the top to meet our girls at the dance. That's was when I was going out with Ivy. My, we had some fun."

"I never thought Duncan was that much of a drinker. I've only known him from in here and he's always been fairly moderate, two or three pints and steady away." Bob's made this observation on several occasions, in fact, the conversation or variations of it have been had on a regular basis over the years, albeit prompted by different circumstances, and have become as comfortable as an old shoe. So comfortable, in fact, that Bob can actually visualise himself in the pub in the city with Fred and Duncan.

"Oh, he could handle it in his younger days. We all could, although he was never as bad as me. When I got back to England, I had that much back pay you wouldn't believe it.

And I spent every penny on beer." Fred grins as he says this. "Although you're right, Duncan was always more of a dancer, and didn't the girls love him. He used to twirl Ivy around and I used to think, better watch that one."

"Not worried, were you? The question is a mock one as Bob knows there wouldn't have been anything going on, but the thought they may have been adds a certain spice to the conversation for the old men."

"Not in the slightest. Even if he could have swayed Ivy, we were mates in those days and it wouldn't have crossed his mind to try. Although I must admit there were a lot of men breathed easier when he married Ruby."

"Ruby will be taking it badly. I always thought they were a strange pair but they seem to have stuck together." And a strange pair they do seem. Duncan is as easy going as Ruby is driven, as mellow as Ruby is fierce, as soft as Ruby is hard. Nobody has a bad word for Duncan and nobody has a good one for Ruby. On many occasions, the maxim 'opposites attract' has been applied to them and on every occasion the inference has been 'how did he end up with her?' But this isn't really fair, the easy-going manner that endeared Duncan to people also made him the philanderer he was, and putting up with his philandering probably contributed to what she was. Her hardness often originated from his actions. And yet she loved him, had fought the other girls for him when he was the master of the dance hall and jack the lad. He knew she loved him unequivocally, as he always crawled back to her after his peccadilloes. People said it might have been different if they'd had children but others said it was just as well they hadn't.

"Aye. No doubt Ivy will be popping around to see her. They used to be good mates when they were girls and Ivy still likes her. Although I must admit I can't see why. She wasn't very nice to her years ago. Always thought that she was after Duncan. Even when we started stepping out, she was suspicious."

"Ruby was suspicious of everyone. Not that she didn't have a good right to be in most cases," Bob's comment brings a few laughs around the table. The men laugh at Ruby being cuckolded because they know that Duncan would never have deserted her and that her manner deserved it.

"Speaking of Ivy, is she picking you up later?" This is another regular question. Fred lives two miles away and since they tightened up the drink driving laws, and more recently with his declining health, his wife has ferried him to and from the pub every Tuesday and Thursday and Sunday in December. Prim and proper behind the wheel, meticulous with her manoeuvres, Fred wouldn't dare to criticise her driving. He had when she'd first started, but had received short shrift in return and learned to mind his manners since. Everyone considered Fred to be a hard man but if they thought he was the master in his own house they were sadly mistaken.

"Yes, she'll be along at nine. She's a good un." And nine it will be, not a minute before and not a minute after. On the dot, the car will appear opposite the pub, execute an exact turn in the school entrance and, paying due care to oncoming traffic, cross the road and coast to the door. Fred will have been watching for her for five minutes, even though she's never a minute early or a minute late, and will rush to leave the pub, his drink finished five minutes earlier, the glass left balanced on the edge of the table.

The conversation drifts between the mundane and silence, the silence often being the most companionable, when they don't feel the need to fill the empty spaces in the conversation. At this point, they become merely three old men who've known each other for years and who are happy in each other's company, where reputations have been established and don't need to be fought over. It's with this feeling, companionship and contentment, that Fred looks at his watch at twenty to nine and concentrates on finishing his drink, the glass comfortable only a third full.

Chapter Two

At nine, Fred is nursing his empty glass, staring out of the window as the car, with Ivy at the wheel, pulls up. The glass goes on the table as he shouts goodnight and rushes to the door, slightly flustered as if he's late and expecting a reprimand. There is nothing strange there, except that anyone who has known and worked with him knows he has never taken a reprimand in his life. This is the man who famously went in front of an interview board, told them what they were doing was stupid and still got the job. But flustered he is. Half walking, half jogging the short distance between the pub and the car he opens the passenger door and jumps in, shutting the door smartly as he does.

"Haven't kept you waiting, have I, dear?"

"Of course, you haven't, I've just pulled up." The question is pointless, the answer sharp, and the conversation a standard that is repeated twice a week and three times in December. It's not a conversation; it's a ritual, an act of contrition and an acknowledgement of who is in control. Fred is aware that the decision to be there is Ivy's, that she could be late or not turn up if she wanted to and that she is in his life on her terms. Most people would not understand the exchange, but then it isn't meant for other people's hearing and they will not hear it. It represents a legacy that has taken root over the years and now dictates the actions of those involved.

"Did you have a good time?" Ivy's tone would suggest that she doesn't care whether Fred has had a good time or not. But in her own way, she does care; Fred's welfare has, over the years, become her major concern and her reason for existing. At first, she had lavished her attention on her son, the doting mother living through her child. But he had become a man, had left home and forged his own live. And she was glad for him, to see him upstanding and competent as she had intended. She liked to believe she had been even handed with him, balancing love with discipline, instilling respect in him whilst teaching him the world was a hard place. And she had succeeded admirable. He admired her, respected her, and in his own way loved her. And because of this, he rarely came home. So that now there was just Fred and her.

"Not bad. The usual crowd was in. Some bad news, however. Apparently, Duncan isn't very well. Bob was wondering if you'd be seeing Ruby."

There is a barely perceptible wobble on the steering: Duncan is ill. As Fred talks, Ivy is also transported back to those early days and the dances in the city. She too sees the debonair Duncan laughing and swirling the girls around the dance floor. She also remembers being swirled around by him. But in those days, Ivy thought him just a bit too much of a handful and had as deftly refused his invitations as she had removed his hands from places they shouldn't have been when they were dancing. She'd warned her friend, Ruby, what he was like but to no avail. Ruby had her sights set on him and that was that. For good or bad, for better or for worse. Poor Ruby.

Anyway, she'd had her sights set on Fred who, in those days, had been something of a catch; handsome, good background, fair prospects and a war hero to boot. His drinking didn't seem a problem then; yes, he always had to drink too much on the night but she could wean him off it. Besides, he was never a nasty drunk; always everyone's friend until laughter ceased and he passed out to sleep it off. The young don't look wrecked by drink, and it never affected him the next day. But marriage had taught her that it wasn't the drink that was the problem but what it was hiding that was.

It was the screaming that woke her, the thrashing that scared her and his reluctance to talk about it that depressed her. Lying there, during the early days of their marriage, she had tried to restrain him. On the first occasion, she'd managed to wake him but later, he'd lashed out in his sleep, fought her off, bruised her body and strained her emotions. She knew that now they'd call it posttraumatic stress disorder; the accumulated horrors that had been suppressed only to rise to the surface when the traumas had disappeared. But in those days, it was, especially to Fred, a sign of weakness. And that was something that Fred couldn't live with, was of the wrong generation to cope with and which very nearly drove them apart. When she'd tried to talk to him, he'd clammed up, when she'd persisted; he'd grown angry and when she'd asked him to seek help, he'd flown into a rage, gone out on a two-day bender and returned drunk, battered and covered in vomit. She hadn't asked him again about it for some time.

However, the silence had not helped. Not only did it create a barrier between them but it meant they couldn't tackle the root problem causing it. As the nightmares and screaming raged and the thrashing continued, she was driven from her own bed and from then on, they slept separately. They still did, but now, it was because they were both used to it and too old to change. And it had never affected her son. The boy had merely assumed, fed by American films, that all couples had single beds and that when their mother resorted to the spare room. It was in protest at his father's snoring. By the time he was old enough to wonder, the nightmares had gone.

But in the early days of their marriage, it had almost broken her. She'd needed help and didn't know which way to turn. It was pointless approaching family; Fred would have found out and never forgiven her for betraying secrets, for exposing his weaknesses. There was no professional counselling in those days and only a weak chinned and elderly vicar to tend to her spiritual needs. And so, she'd turned to Duncan, his friend and another soldier. And that simple cry had led her friend, Ruby, into a rage and fuelled accusations that she couldn't handle and had driven them apart. But that was in the past.

"Yes, I'll pop in and see Ruby tomorrow," Ivy grimaces as she says it. She knows it won't be an easy visit. Over the years, Ruby has fostered a belief that she has been badly done by in life and now, in her old age, it has become the dominant feature of her personality. She sees everything as a personal affront and, in her view, every silver cloud had a dark lining.

"Good girl, I knew we could rely on you."

You always have, she thought. But then again, the comment was typical of Fred. He was the absolute expert at getting people to do things for him, the perfect manager. In his younger days, he'd done it by a mixture of authority and bullying. As he'd grown older, he'd gone for the friendly approach. All his minions were good lads and lasses, patted on the shoulder as they'd done his will. And done it they had, because to be in favour was highly desirable and to be out of favour was as good as requesting a transfer. Now he changed again, becoming literally the old soldier to whom everyone was lovely and did his will to please the old man.

"Can I get you anything when we get in?" The question, like everything else on a Tuesday and Thursday, rarely alters.

"A cup of Horlicks would be nice." The answers inevitably the same. The only thing that stops Ivy from screaming is the fact that he's doing as she has trained him to do. As part of his night time regime, he has a hot milky drink. She'd made him drink one initially as part of her plan to relax him and make him sleep. She isn't sure whether it worked, but as the nightmares stopped, he'd associated it with a calm night's rest and now it had become something of a placebo for him. With the drink, he slept soundly, without it he paced the floor.

"I'll get it for you." As Fred wanders through the hall and into the lounge, Ivy hangs up her coat and puts on her slippers, neatly placing her shoes in the rack where the slippers had been. Shoes are always racked; no matter how many people are in the house, the rack is never overflowing and when there are only the two of them, it is never empty. It retains a used look courtesy of her household management. The management is such that Fred never even notices it; his world is now one of simple contentment. A cosseted life that involves a little gardening, the reading of books and a drink with friends twice a week and three times in December. It's a life he assumes he shares with his friends but in that he is also wrong.

Chapter Three

After Fred leaves, Bob and Alex enjoy another drink; In Bob's case, another pint of beer whist Alex nurses a whiskey. Bob has never lost his taste for beer and has the additional pint each night he meets his friends but his enjoyment, even after all these years, is spoilt by the fact that he thinks it marks him as common, as if you can take the man from the colliery but you can't take the colliery from the man. To the casual observer, or even the knowledgeable observer, this is not apparent as Bob actually comes across as an assertive, confident, perhaps bigoted individual. But behind the assertiveness lurks a fear he has learned to live with but never banish, a fear that what he has will be taken from him and he'll be sent back to where he came from. In some ways, it has soured his enjoyment of life, or perhaps the souring of his life has given him this perception. But he doesn't rationalise it in this way and this means he can never abandon his public beliefs, even when they seem strange even to him.

Bidding farewell, Bob leaves the pub to walk home. There is no lift for him; even if Joan could drive, she would be unlikely to collect him. It's not that she objects to his drinking, like him she grew up in the colliery and accepts that men drink. Nor is it because of any animosity, such a petty act wouldn't cross her mind. Nor is it because she is lazy, in her own way, she's industrious around the house. It's more that it isn't in her mind set that she should or could pick him up so it wouldn't become an issue. Joan has a fixed idea on what is expected of her and that doesn't include intruding on a man's world. To the world at large, this would appear to suit Bob, the bigoted man with the little woman at home. But years before he would have liked something different.

Besides, the walk is a short one. Leaving the main door, he crosses over the road to the school entrance where half an hour earlier Ivy had turned to pick up Fred. The school, like the pub sits in the middle of the estate. Or rather it sits on the main street that the estate was built around. Forty years earlier, this little street of terraced houses, pub and chapel had been a small, self-contained village but that changed in the sixties when the housing boom took off. It still likes to think of itself as a village and, in many ways, it is, the thousand or so houses that make it up have been settled for two and three generations, people have grown old here and it has a history. But it still retains elements of the new and a sixties brashness that no amount of makeovers can eradicate. It is exactly what it seems, pleasant suburbia with a semi-rural aspect.

Bob turns at the school and walks along to the entrance of the estate proper, the long link road that circles around the estate and provides access for all the residents. It also sets the tone of the estate, with its neat semis interspaced with larger detached, the two dwellings set apart by both size and different roof designs. The buildings are now getting dated, but to Bob, they still look as new as the day he moved in. It only seems like yesterday but it was nearer forty years ago, when he was a young man, the sixties were in full swing and anything seemed possible. It was when you were convinced the world was going to change for the better and the old order would be banished. Bob had embraced this with the rest of his generation, still moulded by his upbringing to be a worker, and proud of it, but also to expect to be rewarded for it. Free love had passed him by, he was already married with a young family, but he wanted the rest of what the sixties had to offer and that was material. The estate captured for him this new dream, its open plan a contrast to the narrow lanes with high back walls in which he'd grown up. Space for him represented progress.

Things had been different then. He hadn't been any more relaxed when he was younger; what was now disappointment fuelled into anger was then ambition turned into drive. Long days at work were followed by nights at college and weekends on overtime. But his expectations had been greater, Joan had been his and the future had been bright. Was it the failure of the future to deliver their dreams that had changed Joan or had it been him? Or had it been they'd never had anything in common and time had merely emphasised that.

Bob turns the corner into his own street, a cul-de-sac of ten houses off the main link. He gazes, as he always does, at his house standing on its own in the corner, offset from its two neighbours. He's still proud it of but has, for a long time, denied himself any pleasure from this. The windows and frames gleam, the lawns are neatly clipped, gutters are cleared and even the drains have been flushed. The industry he put into his job and getting on he now puts into his chores. Even the car, now safely ensconced in the garage, is immaculate. The only thing missing from the house is light coming from it and any sense that it is lived in.

When the children had been at home, it blazed, to his consternation, with light and noise. Now there is only a slight glow from the sitting room where he knows Joan will be sitting in the semi darkness watching TV. He lets himself in with his key; the front door is never left unlocked these days, and turns on the hall light as he hangs up his coat. "Is that you?" Joan's voice calls from the lounge. He suppresses a scowl, if it wasn't what kind of answer would she expect. Many years ago, he would have answered 'no, it's the burglar' but now he can't be bothered. Secretly, he thinks she is stupid, but it wasn't always like that and he still, in his own way, loves her.

Joan is sitting in front of the TV as he goes into the lounge. A small woman she's not fat but her lack of interest in her appearance gives her body an overall shapelessness. She's sitting hunched in the chair, eyes glued to the screen, living the scene with the characters. Bob can't get into the programmes but doesn't begrudge her the pleasure she takes from them as it leaves him free to do his own things. Once they'd done things together but it is as if they've both forgotten that. Now, they go through the motions.

"Any news from the pub?" She'd used to say gossip but this had brought no response so now she asks for the news.

There rarely is and she's not really interested, but it maintains a fiction of conversation.

"Not really." Joan hasn't been in the pub for years and has long since lost touch with the people who go in. For their generation, it's very much a man's preserve. "Oh, Duncan's not very well apparently. You remember him, don't you?" As Bob says it, Joan turns quickly around.

"What's wrong with him?" there's concern in her voice and an animation in her movements.

"Cancer, I think." Bob is a little surprised by her interest. "I didn't think you knew him that well."

"Of course, I do. Have you forgotten that he and Ruby used to live just down the road when we first moved here?" Bob has forgotten, like all the men in the pub he's known them so long that histories are forgotten. And they haven't got together as couples for so long that he doesn't associate them with Joan at all.

"That was a long time ago." Bob is searching his memory and starts to recall the time. It was shortly after they had moved to the estate, when Neil was a toddler and Joan was expecting Gillian. Then they'd been happy. They'd worked hard for the deposit for the house, there wasn't a lot left over but enjoyment was cheap: a few friends, a pack of beers and a bottle of sherry. Bob has forgotten what Joan was like in those days. Always small she'd been a pretty little thing, petite but feminine, not brash but full of fun. It was what had attracted him to her. She was different from the other girls in the village.

Seven years younger than him, she'd grown up when he'd been doing his National Service. She'd been working in the department store, and he'd talked to her when he'd gone to get the bus home. She was better than the rest and like him had wanted to move out and forward. And so, they'd courted, and saved, and bought their first house when no one else was buying, and having made their money on it, moved to the estate. And here, they had come into their own, mixing with people like themselves, avoiding the clubs and pubs, drinking in each other's houses and fraternising within a small group. And Duncan and Ruby had been at the centre of that crowd, the hosts, older than the others and, with no children, better off. Or rather Duncan had been the centre of the crowd, Ruby was only friendly with the men and those women she felt weren't flirting with Duncan. And with Duncan, that didn't leave many. It was that that had broken the group, shortly after which the couple had moved.

"Didn't they move under a bit of a cloud? Something to do with some woman?" Bob has known Duncan for so long that it's not so much that he's forgiven him his sins but that, like the rest, he's accepted Duncan for what he is. And at the end of the day, he is charming, men value his friendship and women had always wanted him. Even as an old man, he was charming.

"That was just Ruby. You know how she was. Nobody ever proved anything but she was always suspicious." Joan is scowling as she says this. Bob remembers when she didn't scowl, when she had liked people.

"Strange." Bob is remembering other things. Rumours that have circulated over the years. "You know, I was with Fred tonight and he mentioned that he'd ask Ivy to call in and see Ruby. And yet a lot of people always said that Ivy was Duncan's girl. Not that that matters these days." Bob feels a little disloyal about saying this but is also curious as he's always seen Ivy as a dry old stick.

"Don't be silly, Duncan was never the one for Ivy." Her conviction is such that he instantly believes her. It is only much later, as he is lying awake in bed, that he wonders about her conviction that Ivy wasn't the source of the trouble with Duncan and also that if she wasn't the one then did this imply someone else was? But at the time, it doesn't occur and he lets the conversation end.

But Joan is happy to let the conversation end as well, lost in her own thoughts. She is well aware of what Bob thinks of her than he is of what she thinks of him. With an intuition he doesn't possess, she knows he is too preoccupied to consider that other people do have thoughts, opinions and desires. But he'd always been like that, totally focussed on what he wanted. When they'd been younger, she'd found that attractive, his desire to get on had set him apart from others in their village, his certainties of where he was going gave him a confidence they couldn't match. But as they'd got older, she'd come to believe that the certainties with which he viewed life were merely an expression of his selfishness and that the confidence he'd shown was little more than bigotry. She was aware that he thought of her as stupid and that they didn't talk anymore because of her absorption in television. But she didn't talk to him anymore because she had nothing to say, and because it was easier not talking as talking and listening to garbage as talking and getting into an argument. She was aware that this was a cop out but she was worn out and couldn't be bothered.

It hadn't always been like that and she wasn't sure when it had happened. It would be easy to say it was when the children had left, that only then had the gulf that had been steadily growing been revealed. But she knew this wasn't true and that her absorption in the family had been as much a reaction to the situation as the development of the love of her children. She'd ceased to think of it and had become absorbed in her own lethargy, sinking deeper into her own pit. But Bob's comment tonight had brought it all to the surface and slammed the fact in front of her that they'd drifted into this situation.

She hadn't seen Duncan for years. She knew that he still went, or had gone, to the pub occasionally and that Bob had spoken to him but as a couple they no longer mixed and her only contact was by Christmas card. Because of this Duncan had, in her memory, been getting younger with each year she hadn't seen him. She knew he was an old man but, in her thoughts, he remained a man in his early forties and in his prime. Which was how he'd been when she'd first met him.

Was that over forty years ago? In her memory, it was still crystal clear but it also seemed part of a different life. The person she'd been then seemed a stranger to her, someone who couldn't have existed. Her memory was tainted by awareness of what she was now: she was not one of those people who still thought of themselves as young and behaved accordingly no matter how ridiculous they looked. Or maybe they were the lucky ones, too ignorant of other people's opinions to be affected by them and free to enjoy themselves. She'd never wanted to be like that but resented what she had become.

She could see herself now, slim in her mini skirt, flirting with Duncan who had the charm of the devil and a reputation to match. But his charm was because you knew he was prepared to gamble on being with you and the devil because he had. But he also knew how to treat women and genuinely liked them and there weren't many in their circle like that. And Duncan loved life, was infectious in his lust for it, and carried you with him.

Despite herself, Joan smiles as the memories transport her back to those times, when the sun is shining, she's young and happy and the world was a wonderful place to live in. In her mind's eye, there, in the garden, all their friends, including Duncan and Ruby, Fred and Ivy and, over in the corner, in the background, Alex. She puzzles momentarily over that thought, as she recalls that Alex always seemed to be there but always on the boundary or in the distance, with the crowd, but not part of it.

Chapter Four

Alex is still like this. As usual, he is the last to leave the pub, but this means he doesn't have to make a fuss and say a lot of goodbyes; he can slip away without people noticing. He's the kind of man who, when asked, will invoke the response 'yes, he was in earlier but he must have gone!' But he doesn't invite sympathy, that's the way he likes it and people seem to appreciate this. And so, in his usual manner, he leaves quietly by the front door, the shortest route with the least chance of being noticed. He, too, crosses the road to where Ivy turned the car, pausing wistfully before turning left and heading down the original main street.

Unlike the majority of others in the pub, Alex doesn't live on the estates but in an old house on the main street, mixed in with the old terrace of colliery houses dating back to the nineteenth century. But his house is substantial, double fronted and possessing a courtyard to the rear where the doctor who built it used to keep his trap in the days before cars. The fact it opens on to the main road belies its interior elegance. Like its owner, its real characteristics are hidden, as if its essence is defined not by what it reveals but by what it conceals.

Alex lets himself into the hall and flicks the lights on revealing a long hall still floored with the original Victorian tiles. The elegance is faded, but all the more attractive for it. In its original state, it has gone from quality, through to old fashioned, to modern desirability and elegance in ignorance of trends. It remains what it was intended to be; solid, stylish and dependable. A Victorian hat stand in the corner complements the hall and Alex hangs his coat and walking stick on it. With the exception of an umbrella, it is empty of other items, testifying both to Alex's status as a bachelor and his neat existence. Like the rest of the house everything is in its place and, if not recently decorated, meticulously clean, testament to his habits and the endeavour of the woman whose been coming twice a week for the past ten years.

The sitting room opens off to the right of the hall and Alex turns here and enters the room already lit by a standard lamp operated by a timer. It's the only light he uses in the room; during the day the south facing room catches the daylight and during the evening he prefers the gentle subdued light the lamp provides. His chair is positioned near it, accompanied by a table to hold his glass or cup depending on the time of day. Now he goes to the sideboard in the corner and fills the glass already there from the decanter next to it. It's not a large measure but a good malt tasting all the better from being served from the decanter into cut glass. It's a practice he picked up from his father, always taking the trouble over the ritual to add to the pleasure. Sitting back in his chair he takes a sip from the whiskey, places the glass on the table and leans back with his eyes closed. He feels pleasantly weary rather than tired and enjoys the sensation, the physical depletion gentling the mind as he ruminates on the day. It has been a funny day, he thinks, part old safe routine and part reflection. Of course, it's Duncan that's triggered this.

In his mind's eye, Alex is now back in time. Bizarrely, the picture he is conjuring up is the same one Joan is contemplating, the scene in Duncan's garden when they'd all first been friends; Duncan and Ruby holding court, Bob and Joan so very young, Fred and Ivy already set in their ways. And him, watching, always watching. He's on his own, has been for many years since he'd lost his wife. She'd been tragically young but he doesn't dwell on that now. He's never remarried and can't really remember now what it was like to share his life. There was someone else after his wife, but that was not to be as she was already married and couldn't leave her husband. He understood why, he was of the old school, and accepted it and so had learnt to enjoy what little time they had, to cherish being near her and accept that most of his life would be as it had been; ordered, measured, unremarkable but above all, calm.

There has been a time when he'd been passionate. It is a word that is now, in his opinion, misused to describe nothing better than flagrant promiscuity or excuse wild behaviour. His behaviour had never been wild; his father would not have allowed it, but he had believed in rightness of things and had possessed an immense appetite for life, taking part enthusiastically in sports and being the centre of a large crowd of friends. His all boys school had given way to an all male college at Oxford where the beliefs he'd had had been further refined till he was the epitome of a young English gentleman that the country relied on. And then the war had come and that had all ended. But he rarely thinks of that anymore. Over the years, he's existed within the haven he's created for himself, accepted what he's been given, not striving for anymore, his life measured, no excitement but no more pain, hopes not held, so disappointments managed. But he thinks wistfully, things could have been different.

Chapter Five

Everyone thinks things could have been different, especially Ruby. Ruby's life should have been simple; all she had to do was look after the man she adored and be happy. But as much as she looked after Duncan, happiness eluded her. It wasn't that Duncan treated her badly; he was as charming with her as he was with everyone else, as much fun with her as with everyone else. But that was the thing that caused her the most distress, she wanted to be special but Duncan couldn't seem to treat her in that way. She'd come to realise that he couldn't treat anyone else in that way either but that provided little solace, he was everyone's friend, but no one got close to him. She now knew, after all the years, that she'd never been in danger of him leaving her but the bitter pill was realising that if she had gone, he wouldn't have missed her.

Duncan literally lived for the minute; there was no room for doubts, no room for worry and no cares for the future. Because of that everyone loved him but because of that he seemed to love no one. She wondered if they'd had children if it would have been different but doubted it and as time went by, the desire for a family had died; she'd had one child to look after and that was enough. Because that, in many ways, was what Duncan was. Highly capable, independent, likeable he was also an emotional cripple, another victim of the war. All his women eventually realised that, when the initial passion subsided, they quickly realised there was nothing there and drifted away. And that was why there was never any danger in him leaving, because when the affair died, she was still there, the one person who never left and therefore, the one person he stayed with.

There had only been one occasion when she'd had any doubts that he would go, and that was not because of Duncan but because she recognised in the woman another person prepared to put up with him. But the woman had other commitments, had painfully seen the truth and stopped that affair. Then she had put the matter out of the way by insisting they move house and for once, he'd capitulated. But she'd lost because of it, not seeing her friends and suffering loneliness.

All her friends had not deserted her however. Earlier that morning, she'd received a phone call from Ivy who was now coming to see her. Ivy, her oldest friend. It was funny to look at it in that perspective, because being her oldest friend, Ivy had always been there. And, because she'd always been there, it meant that she was the one person who knew what everyone had done. Or thought she did because Ruby was convinced there were skeletons that even she didn't know about. But she was looking forward to seeing her and, in fact, needed to see her. Not only because she was the person she was most comfortable with but because she was the only real connection she still had with her past.

Her past. Everyone thought that they knew her but they knew nothing. Those who went back far enough, to the dances in the city, assumed that she and Ivy had been girlhood friends and had grown up together. And because they'd assumed that, they'd assumed that they'd had the same background that she'd been comfortably well off and drifted into that crowd with her. And that she'd met Duncan there. But that was far from the truth, but only Ivy knew that. But the car was pulling up; Ruby can see it through the net curtains, outside the house. A neat little car for the neat little woman getting out of it. Ruby watches her going down the path to the front door. She can see Ivy but knows, from practice, that Ivy can't see her through the curtains. So, she waits for the bell to ring before getting up to answer the door, so that no one can think she's waiting for a visitor.

When the front door opens, Ivy has the advantage. The sun shining behind her dazzles Ruby but also lights her perfectly for Ivy's inspection. The view is not heart-warming; Ivy sees a painfully thin woman, lines of pain etched in a gaunt face with lips appearing to be pressed into a permanent grimace. Everything about her is tense, like a coiled spring that is only held together by the slenderest of threads that constitute the sinews of her body. Instead of frailty, however, age had given her a semblance of toughness, like old leather that is cracked and misshapen but so hard it is unlikely ever to split. It does, in fact, match what she is, a fragile creature covered in an unbreakable shell.

The vision doesn't shock Ivy; she has seen it develop over the years, but it does sadden her to see her friend like this. Because, despite everything, she does still consider them friends. They go back too far for that to ever change. So far back that their lives are intertwined and integral to each other, but over such a long-time frame that it's as if they've lived several different lives together. Now they're two old women together but it doesn't seem too long since they were young girls. No, Ivy corrects herself, she was a young girl but Ruby always had an edge, even then.

"Are you coming in on are you going to stand there gawping?"

Despite her pleasure at seeing her friend, Ruby is unable to cut the sarcasm from her voice. She regrets it, but it's too ingrained for her to either stop it before or to apologise after. So, she turns her back and walks down the hall, giving the impression she doesn't care whether Ivy follows her or not but hoping all the while that she does. Ivy watches as she walks away, looking at the narrow back and the surprisingly still shapely legs before she follows. Ruby always did have good legs; they were her best feature and she smiles at the thought as she remembers her efforts to secure nylons to properly show them off. That had been just at the end of the war when they'd first met, working in one of the offices that linked the armed forces to the top brass and the politicians. Not that she'd seen much cloak and dagger; she'd been a young girl hired to type and file but excited at being involved in the war effort.

Ruby was already in the office when she'd arrived. Only two years older but already wise to the way things were run and already showing the toughness that would later consume her. But she'd never taken that out on the young Ivy, but had taken her under her wing, showing her what was required, covering her early mistakes, protecting her from reprimand and shielding her from the attentions of the military men who passed through. She was under no illusions about who could be trusted, who could be flirted with and who had to be avoided.

She'd drummed it into the young Ivy that once her reputation slipped, she would never be able to reclaim it and would become a target for every randy soldier around. Young as she was, Ivy had realised that reputation was everything to Ruby and that no one got to chink her amour. Her past was unknown, her present vague and her ambitions secret. She was the efficient and standoffish secretary so essential to the military. That was until a young officer called Duncan had appeared in the office one day.

"How's Duncan?" Ivy asks as she follows Ruby into the sitting room. The room is spotless; Ruby runs her house the way she used to run her offices, with cool efficiency. But the room, whilst clean, lacks any softness.

"Fading." The answer is stark and simple. They could have been discussing the weather but Ivy sees the pain. Ruby sits on the couch and Ivy joins her, instinctively taking both her hands in hers. Ruby goes to pull away, in her characteristic manner, then stops, folds and the tears of years fall as she clings to her friend.

"What did the doctors say?"

"What do they ever say? That he's as comfortable as can be expected and that he's in no pain. Then, when you nag at them about hope, they say there's always hope and change the subject. But now, they're not even saying there's hope, they've started on about being brave. What the buggers really mean is he's on the way out but they won't come out and say it."

Ivy is shocked. All the friends know Duncan is ill, and they all know too well that at their age what can start as a minor illness can quickly turn into something terminal. But it has been fast and none of them have come to terms that, in his case, it could be the end. They've seen enough friends go and become somewhat inured to it but this is Duncan. Duncan has always seemed to be indestructible, going through the entire war whilst all around him men were dying, never having a day's illness in his life, bounding with energy and always the first for a prank and a laugh. Ivy knows the rest of the crowd felt that they shared his invulnerability but if Duncan is to go what of the rest.

"How's Duncan taking it?" Ivy knows that now she begins to feel if he is to die then the rest of them are next.

"As Duncan takes everything else. He accepts what life has to give him and no more. Perhaps that's his trouble; he's never had any fear but never had any hope." Ivy says this as if she doesn't wish to believe it which inevitably means she does. But she's wrong about that, Duncan did used to have hope, but that was a long time ago.

At that moment, Duncan is lying in bed. He's quite comfortable lying in bed, his body feels weightless and the sheets mould around his body almost sensuously. There's no pain; part of his mind tells him that's because they've just administered his drugs, and because of that no anxiety. Sunshine through the open curtains bathes his body in both light and warmth and he's experiencing an almost spiritual feeling. Well almost, because Duncan's never been spiritual with anything unless it came out of a bottle. And he's had a lot of experience with that. And with anything else that relied upon the senses. He's thinking that now as he watches the young nurse, three beds away leaning over, straightening the bed that awaits a new patient. He's not experiencing any stirring in his loins, that familiar feeling that's informed his life and provided the distractions from the more mundane. Not that he's ever been dominated purely by the act.

No, Duncan is one of those men who genuinely appreciates a woman's beauty, who, even now, is enjoying the way the fabric of her dress is stretching across her buttocks and riding up her thigh. He's noticing the pretty legs and the way her calves arch against the slightly raised shoes. To Duncan, there is no greater beauty than the female form and he's wallowed in it all his life, has surrendered to it as often as possible and worshipped at its temple. Yes, it can truly be said that Duncan loves the female body. But it could also be said that he doesn't love women. Beauty may only be skin deep but Duncan has never dug below that.

And so, he lies there in a kind of contentment, feeling the warmth seep through his body whilst the sight in front of him stimulates his mind. That stimulation could be profound if he thought to pursue it but he doesn't. The memories it invokes aren't critically examined, but merely enjoyed. The dress riding up looks almost sixties in its style and the bottom it encases reminiscent of one of his conquests. So sharp is the memory that he can practically feel the flesh, smell the musk and taste the sweat. Duncan not only appreciates the sight of the female form but also the woman smell that accompanies it. He remembers the willingness of his conquest, the ardour in which she responded and the abandon of her orgasm. All the more surprising as she looked a slip of an innocent girl. No, not innocent as she was married, but innocent in that you didn't expect her to take such pleasure in the flesh.

The warmth and sunlight, the sixties dress and the memory of the conquest takes him back to a summer long ago, during the long June days, standing in the garden with friends drinking and laughing. It was when he was in his prime, less than twenty years after the war and before he reached middle age. When he was still considered the dashing war hero and when such heroes were wanted. And if he was wanted, who was he to deny his public. Because public they were.

The fifties had mainly been austere. Yes, they'd had some fun, but everything was always in short supply, even if you had money, and there was drabness around. The weekends in the city had been okay but they were tempered by the survival of the week, and for every decent night of weather there had been the nights when it was cold or impermeably wet. He knew Fred looked back on it with pleasure but in those days, he was rarely sober so he was no judge. Ivy was fun, however. He thinks wistfully of her, so innocent, so desirable but back then so unobtainable. And so, chaperoned by Ruby.

Duncan had no qualms about cheating on Ruby but would never flaunt it in her face and to have chased Ivy then would have been unforgivable. He had never questioned whether or not he loved Ruby. He knew he needed her which might have meant that he did, but he didn't mind having other women which probably meant that he didn't. But, then again that was too much thought and he avoided that at all costs.

And so, he's back in the garden. His friends around him, the centre of attention, which was where he liked being, and sinfully chasing women and counting the conquests which fed his ego and made him feel better than the others. Because in a way he had never really made friends; not in the true sense of the word. He was never short of company: in fact, his company was sought. And if he was in any trouble, he could always count on any number of people to bail him out, no questions asked. People cared for him; they were his friends but he wasn't theirs. The truth was that he enjoyed being with them but if they weren't there then he would have enjoyed being with someone else. Duncan was a walking contradiction; because he wasn't interested in becoming involved with people, he could satisfy his curiosity about them. And this, in turn, led them into an intimacy where they became his friends without realising there was nothing coming in return except his company when they sought it.

Duncan hadn't always been like that. At school, he'd been quiet and studious, and even in his later years, no one would deny his sharp intelligence. But the quiet, shy boy who loved his books was no longer there. The adolescent so desperate to fit in had disappeared. The young man so full of hope was gone. In a lucid moment, he'd been watching Jarman's Caravaggio, not because he liked the story but because he was always impressed by the photography and visual brilliance. What had struck him was when the young Caravaggio has a knife whose blade bears the legend 'no hope' on one side but 'no pain' on the other. That had, momentarily summed it up for him; no hope but no pain, what you lost for what you gained.

But enough of that, the nurse is shifting position, leaning over the bed and facing him, twisting slightly to straighten a pillow so that her top clings and shapes her breast. Out of the corner of her eye, she sees Duncan watching and flashes him a smile, mistaking his observation as that of an old man bored and seeking attention. She's far too young to believe that a man of his age can still observe a woman in sexual terms and, when she often stops to talk with him, sees merely a charming old man. But this is just another role that Duncan has assumed, progressing from the dashing young officer, the rakish hero, the experienced older man to the gentle old gentleman. But Duncan's roles are created for him alone, to allow him to function, and not to attract anyone too him. Because he doesn't really care.

Chapter Six

Someone who does care is currently pruning back his fuchsia, knelt down on creaking knees as he cuts the bushy stems back. He knows he should cut them further than he does, but his plants seem to grow exceptionally high and he can't bring himself to curb their untamed beauty. A lot of his garden is like that, but its wildness is nurtured and the effect is of a sea of carefully contrived colour and natural shape. His neighbours see Fred's gardening as a pastime that is just that, something he's taken up to pass his time in retirement, but Fred actually likes it, enjoys nature imposing its beauty on a world that is always contriving to be ugly. Fred remembers the scenes of battles where the earth has been gashed and laid bare and yet, when revisited, has been a blaze of colour and growth as nature has reasserted herself.

Fred pushes himself up and puts a hand to the small of his back to help him straighten and ease his aching muscles; or bones as he prefers to think of them. He's long since given up believing he has any muscles left although it hadn't always been like that. In his youth, he'd been incredibly fit and quite the sportsman. Rugby, cricket, running, even football, he took part in them all. What he lacked in skill; having little grace, he'd made up for in strength, phenomenal stamina and a cultivated aggression. These had been the traits that were admired on the playing pitch and Fred had found himself much in demand. And this hadn't displeased him because he had yearned to be accepted. The irony of it was that it helped mask his insecurity, brought on by his disciplinarian father who had no time for boys who were soft and had determined to make a man of him. But where his father couldn't make him aggressive, his longing for friends had the opposite effect.

Although he had a natural aversion to violence, he learned to use controlled brutality on the field, to be one of the boys. And playing rugby, this had been okay. But in the army, it had been different.

Fred had joined up early after the start of the war. Although he could have been an officer, he was happy to be with the men, one of the lads, making him one of them. And making it had been easy; where others struggled physically, he excelled, where others kicked authority, he embraced it, where others were despised, he was admired and he revelled in it. Quickly, he gained a stripe and learned the institutionalised brutality that shaped his relationships from those days onwards. And shape them they did because Fred was a bully, he learned early that people might despise you, might want to get even with you, but in the end, did what you wanted. And men respected you. If someone had stood up to him it might have been different but they never had and the more he got his own way, the easier it became. Professionally, he wasn't liked, but could be relied on to get the job done. But he could live with that and, more importantly, the respect he got in his social life and when drinking with his cronies. He was seen as a hard man and hard men were admired, were courted and had their opinions sought. Nobody knew of the nights he sweated, that he and Ivy had separate beds and he would rather have died than admit that.

Now, it was easier. He was older and had earned the right to be mellow. Now, he could voice strong opinions and not be expected to back them up. He could be forgiven if he was cantankerous and humoured if he wanted to be emotional. For the first time in his life, he could start to touch upon those things he couldn't bear, the thoughts he had pushed to the back of his mind, and confront the ghosts that tormented him. But he couldn't do it consciously and relied on people asking him. But there was enough of the curious to do that, enough cronies to feed him lines.

Fred's main crony is also gardening at this time. His gardening, however, does not recognise beauty so much as order. It's pretty in its way, the heights of plants clearly regimented and the colours dispersed in accordance with all the instructions from all the references books on the subject. It represents all that is commonly regarded as desirable and is, therefore, common. It has life but no soul. This could be said to be how Joan sees Bob, what she took for drive to succeed was merely the determination to be accepted. But not just by anyone, Bob had distinct ideas who was to be valued.

Bob has always been a hero worshipper. He was taught to respect, to admire those who worked hard and who were the pillars of society, to emulate them and use them as the model for his life. If he'd been a little older, he would have served during the war and, if he'd survived, would have seen that all men were affected by it. But he didn't, and therefore, has no experience to judge by. So, he sits in quiet awe of Fred and Duncan and, to a lesser extent, Alex. He's never really known Alex but feels, for reasons he can't quite discern, that he deserves respect. Respect for the quiet confidence he exudes and the lack of any need to promote himself. Or, more precisely, his utter lack of fear.

Fear probably sums it up. Bob has never known a day without fear, from being a small boy to the present day. His father had been a disciplinarian, always hard on him, determined as he said to make a man of him. So, when he was small, he was in fear of his father, at first irrationally and then resentfully. And then he was physically afraid. A small boy, he grew late and was the subject of schoolyard bullies and rough street louts. And as he conquered that fear, becoming physically harder than he either wanted or intended he became afraid of poverty, of losing everything he had. And this eventually translated itself into the absolute fear of failure that now lies at the bottom of his soul.

But now, it is not a fear of failure; it's a deep-seated acceptance that he has failed, but an acceptance he won't admit. He knows he has a nice house, a decent pension, a family and friends but this is not enough. Because even though he can't rationalise it the answer is very simple: because he's always been afraid, he's never been happy and now he doesn't know how to be.

Joan is also not happy although she knows it and also knows why. She's not right but this doesn't help her. She's unhappy because she knows that Bob doesn't love her, that she is past her prime and that there is no future. It isn't true: it's not that Bob doesn't love her but more that he hates himself. But the end result is the same and the relationship is subsequently cold. This is even harder to bear as Joan is, despite looks, a passionate woman. Once she held that passion for Bob, and when that relationship turned cold, she held it for another man. But the other man abandoned her so now she sits and watches.

At the moment, she is watching Bob in the garden, measuring his borders with the precision of a draftsman, straightening them to a standard that would have satisfied a roman engineer. His obsessiveness used to intimidate her and she would try to run the house along his perfectionist lines. Then it had irritated her and she had done the opposite, deliberately throwing towels across the bath and leaving newspapers around until they irritated him.

Now, she no longer cares and he no longer argues about it, she does things her way and he does things his. This effectively means that the inside of the house is hers and the outside is his. She has the kitchen and he has the shed; she has the sitting room and he has the garage. They're like two animals, each with their territory staked out. But they still communicate, in a way, and still function as a couple and as parents to their children. Perhaps they are too tired to fight or maybe there is some deeply hidden love still there. There must be something as she leaves the kitchen to take him his coffee.

"Thanks," he mumbles automatically as she passes him the mug. He takes the mug in one hand and places the other in the small of his back as he straightens, mirroring Fred's actions two miles away. Maybe the coincidence in some strange telepathic way affects him, because as he holds the mug, he surveys the garden and feels dissatisfaction at the arrangements of the plants, seeing their clipped and shaped bodies as being imprisoned rather than ordered. He resists a sudden urge to pull them out and set them free, rationalising that this will only kill them. He frowns at the thought.

"Everything okay?" Joan has seen the scowl and is puzzled by it. Bob rarely smiles but his countenance is usually merely set, displaying no emotion. She finds his noticeable resentment slightly frightening.

"Just this garden, I'm sick of it. Maybe I'll pull it up and have block paving put down. I'm getting too bloody old for this gardening lark anyway!" Joan is now surprised, surprised because Bob is far from too old, surprised because he hates block paving and surprised because he hates any kind of change, anything that detracts from his safe little haven.

"Why don't you? You could put some pots on it, make life easier. There are lots of nice things around." Joan doesn't really care whether he does or doesn't but is now fascinated that he's prepared for change and may be even discussing it.

"That's not a bad idea. Alex has got a cobbled yard with pots and it looks really good. He's got these Greek style pots with topiary in." Joan realises that if Alex has got something similar then there is more chance of Bob doing it. If it had been Fred, he would have felt the same but Joan would have felt bitter about it. But she likes Alex and so she doesn't. She occasionally sees him still in the old high street if she's calling at one of the shops and he always stops, always the old gentleman and always courteous. She thinks it a shame he never married. It's yet another of those mysteries about him. She sighs and goes back inside.

As she is going back into her house, Alex is leaving his. He uses the back door because he's wearing the heavy walking shoes which he leaves in the rear porch of the house so as to not trail mud through. Today, as most days, he is going for his walk, partly to satisfy the demands of the doctor who told him years ago that if he didn't exercise his injured legs, he'd finish crippled with arthritis, partly because it's become a habit but mainly because he enjoys the way the walk and the views of the countryside calm his thoughts and help him accept his lot. He doesn't notice the pots so much admired by Bob as he passes them, they've been there for years and apart from occasionally renewing the shrubs he's oblivious to them. The outside of the house reflects the inside, understated and elegantly faded. Very much like the old gentleman.

Turning the corner of the house, he walks along the wide driveway; or more properly coach way, and emerges onto the high street. Some youths are gathered, children are loitering and he waves to them. They don't wave back, that would be uncool, but they know he's there. He was there when they were smaller, he was there when their parents were children and, in some cases, he was there when their grandparents were children. He's part of their world, he's not frightened by them and so he has their respect. But they won't wave. And so, he walks with their backs to him, up the old high street, left into what is still known as the old estate and then though to the countryside beyond.

On his left, he sees Bob's house, the garden now deserted. But Joan is in at the sitting room window and after a moment, waves to him. He waves back and walks on, wondering about Joan. As much as he drinks with Bob two nights a week and every Sunday in December, he knows that he doesn't keep Joan happy and slightly despises him for it. He was taught that it was a man's duty to keep a woman happy and all his experiences have reinforced that view. But he was never allowed to keep a woman happy for long, nature or propriety always interfering.

Now he's going through the kissing gate; not an ancient device for courting couples but a doubled gate to prevent motorbikes getting through. The lanes and fields beyond are a walker's and dog lovers' paradise but also a continuing attraction for off road bikers. Its late summer and the lanes are still a heady mixture of colour and fragrance, accentuated by the soft light seeping between sheep like clouds. Alex sighs with contentment as he strolls down the path. A part of him is now visiting the past, a place where he is happy.

Chapter Seven

Oxford was always warmer than the rest of the country but the summer before the outbreak of war set a record even for there. Only the rivers offered any comfort and seemed to be permanently full of young students in punts being watched by picnickers lining the banks. In the early evening, the light mellowed, splashing though the trees dappling the water. It added further disbelief to the mounting argument that war was coming and created an almost surreal world that neither denied nor disbelieved what was happening but seemed detached from it. And yet, at the same time, it promised change for many people there and, though they did not know it, an end to a way of life for many.

Alex certainly didn't foresee the end of the current order. He didn't actually see very much and wasn't considered much of a thinker by his fellow students. It wasn't that he was dim; he could often surprise his fellows and students with startling insights during seminars. But these moments of inspiration had no coherence and were ephemeral in nature, unlinked because he couldn't be bothered and because he was academically lazy. Alex was more interested in rugby, cricket, rowing and drinking and carousing with his friends. And in girls. His lecturers had reluctantly concluded that Alex would get a two for intelligence whilst he only deserved a three for effort. But that was fine with Alex.

Academia was far from his mind as he exited Trinity College by the Porter's Lodge and turned left onto Broad Street. It was early evening and he was heading towards the Turf, via the lane opposite Hertford College, for an early evening drink. Not that he couldn't get a drink in college, but that would mean not seeing the pretty young barmaid serving in the low beamed bar. It was a beautiful night, made for romance, he was full of energy and life was sweet. His mood was such that he smiled, despite himself, at the young man staggering under a pile of books, emerging from the gates of Balliol College. Trinity's neighbour, Balliol was also its' arch rival, and rugby matches between the two were hotly, and often violently, contested.

Alex recognised the young man having shared several lectures with him and, more importantly, in his mind, competed against him. Alex was a natural on the sports field, a big committed second row man. He knew that Duncan didn't share his love of the game, and was a reluctant player coerced because their two colleges were amongst the smallest in Oxford, but he also recognised that the boy had talent when he chose to use it. Besides, for some reason, Alex liked him even if he was a bookworm.

He strode up behind Duncan, slapping him on the back and almost making him lose his grip on the tottering pile of books. "And where are you off to young man, as if I didn't know?"

"To the library." There was still a slight trace of the stutter that has once crippled Duncan as a child, which he'd fought and finally conquered, but which had left him withdrawn. "Still got so much to do."

Alex doubted that; he'd seen Duncan at lectures, always prepared, always ready with an answer and always able to see the links that others missed. And in lectures, in an environment he liked, he lost his shyness, his stutter disappeared completely and, lost to himself, his true self came though. Alex found him amusing, this shy boy who could kick on the playing field when need arose and argue bravely with the most formidable professor.

"On a day like today, you must be mad." He put his arm around his shoulder. "Come with me, young man, have a drink and feast your eyes on a vision of true beauty." He began leading him along the road, ducking down the alley that led into the back entrance to the bar.

"I should work," Duncan protested. To Alex, it was strange because it was obvious to everyone but Duncan that he was destined for a first. It was also strange to Alex because he couldn't see the point, College was to be enjoyed, a brief lull before the world became serious, a time to sow wild oats away from home. Another thought occurred to him.

"What's the point? Do you think any of us will be here next year?" It wasn't something he'd thought particularly about. He'd heard the arguments ranging in commons, and couldn't miss the headlines in the papers. But at the moment, they were in the phoney stages, when many believed appeasement would work. And if it wasn't decided yet then there was no point in worrying about it. But he knew that someone like Duncan would be digesting every detail, playing all scenarios and drawing careful conclusions. Besides, it would draw him away from work.

"Do you think the war will come?" Duncan's studious face was all concern and Alex felt momentarily guilty. Then he smiled, if Duncan was worried then it was his duty to cheer him up.

"Maybe, maybe not. Which means let's live for now and forget about it for the moment. Come with your uncle Alex and have some fun." He was now steering them towards the bar door. As if the decision was made, Duncan smiled and began walking with him, no longer resisting the pull forward. Alex laughed and they ducked under the doorway.

The Turf was probably the oldest pub in oxford and certainly had the lowest ceilings. Even short people had to duck to walk across the front bar and negotiate its' narrow corridors. But that's what added character to the place, that and its uneven floors and dark interior. The beer was also exceptionally good.

"What can I get you seeing as I've dragged you into this den of inequity?"

Duncan surveyed the pumps along the bar, looking for something familiar but, not being a drinker, not finding it. He looked up to ask the barman what he recommended and was confronted by two bright blue eyes staring mischievously back at him. They were set in a slightly plump but pretty face that was surrounded by blond curls.

Duncan found it hard to speak but finally managed to stutter, "What do you think?" The girl smiled at his discomfort.

"Try the Abbots," she said, adding cheekily, "it shouldn't be too much for you."

"I'll have one too then, if it's not too much trouble." Alex was leaning across the bar, ostensibly to make himself heard, but more to impress his charms on the lady in question. But for once, his charm didn't seem to be working. Mary, the barmaid, was watching the blushing Duncan who, obviously, only had eyes for her. Alex watched Duncan as Duncan watched Mary as she pulled and placed the two pints on the bar. Alex was obliged to put the money for the drinks on the bar as he took one glass and used his other hand to guide his young companion to a seat near the window. Even here, in the small bay, Duncan sat with his back to the view outside and focussed on the bar where Mary was at work serving another customer. His gaze never wavered and she periodically turned and smiled indulgently, and curiously, at him.

"Careful, she might get the wrong idea with you staring at her like that." Duncan blushed further as Alex said this and looked down into his beer causing Alex to feel sorry for teasing him. It was immediately apparent to him that Duncan had no experience of women and equally apparent that he was totally smitten with Mary with whom he exchanged no more than a few words.

He thought caution might be advisable at this point and warned, "No offence, young man but that one is for fun only."

"What do you mean?" Duncan's tone was, at once, enquiring and pleading but with a belligerent air noticeably in the background. Alex knew that he was going to have to be careful.

"Put it this way, Mary's a good sport. You could say she's a bit of a mascot of the colleges, always with one of the undergraduates. She's fun, not someone to get involved with."

Alex knew, even as he said this, that he was losing ground. It was clear Duncan didn't wish to believe him and that he couldn't be convinced because he wanted to believe otherwise. As Alex watched Duncan's gaze wander back to

Mary who was smiling back at him. Alex decided that nature would run its' course and, who knew, might ultimately do the young bookworm some good.

Twenty years later and that thought came back to Alex. It was 1960, he was again in a bar with Duncan and Fred was there to. This was not unusual as it was a Friday night and traditionally, a night for a drink in the pubs in the old part of town. Tonight, they were in the Bull, not their normal pub, but they'd fancied a change and the Bull had a reputation for good beer. In fact, the reputation was fairly wide spread as the bar was packed to capacity, men standing shoulder to shoulder and cigarette smoke hanging in a pall just below the ceiling. Alex liked a smoke as much as the next man but even his eyes were stinging and he could smell the tobacco in the air.

Duncan, however, seemed oblivious to it, laughing and joking with Fred, his tallness making him stand out in the crowd and his handsome features setting him apart from the rest. Fred marvelled at how these had emerged from the boyish profile of his student days and how he had changed from the bookish youth to the man about town. Of course, he'd pondered this many times before, but tonight, he had been reminded because the girl behind the bar closely resembled Mary, the barmaid of so many years ago.

Of course, she couldn't have been her, this was twenty years on and the girl was no more than in her early twenties. She had the same slightly plump and heavily breasted figure as Mary, the same mischievous look in her eye and the same blonde hair. When she pulled the handle of the beer pump, a lot of eyes followed the way her breasts moved under her dress and Alex had noticed that Duncan's were amongst these. But Duncan was no longer the callow youth, fixated on what he saw. He had given her a quick glance, taken in, at once, her face and figure, smiled briefly then returned to his conversation.

Whereas the Mary of so many years had been flattered by his undivided attention the Mary of that day, if that was her name, was intrigued by the handsome, well dressed and debonair man who had briefly caught her eye. Alex had seen Duncan adopt this strategy on numerous occasions; his seemingly lack of interest a cover for his intentions, a lure for his victims and a prelude to his charm attack. And because he was calculated, he was all the more dangerous. Alex decided to let events again run their course, this time, not to educate the youth, which had been a mistake, but because, this time, he was in no position to either give advice or prevent the inevitable.

His thoughts were interrupted by Duncan himself who leaned over and shouted, "What are you having, Alex, it's my round?"

"Another pint's fine," he replied. He would switch to whisky soon enough but for the moment, he was enjoying the beer. His watch told him that there would be time for one more round and also told him that if Duncan was going to make a move, now was the time he would make it. He watched as he walked towards the bar, seeming to move through the crowd without being touched by the press in the room, a smile already on his lips and the barmaid's eye already caught.

It was a private joke that if it was busy, you always sent Duncan to the bar, as he never failed to get served instantly. He knew he had charm and looks and traded on them unashamedly. Alex had seen it all before but was still fascinated by the performance. He watched as her head came forward, as the smile touched her lips and as the laughter came. Duncan's head then came forward, and he whispered secretively in her ear, reaction spreading across her face as she blushed, drew back, then laughed again and hit him softly on the shoulder, an unconvincing rebuke for his cheek. He laughed in reply and, picking up the drinks, returned to Alex and Fred.

"Looks like we're walking again, Fred," Alex said before Duncan was in earshot.

He didn't really mind the walk as he enjoyed the exercise and it was a warm night. What he actually hated was covering for Duncan, who would lie to Ruby that he was late because he had dropped the chaps off. If he was especially late, he would concoct the tale 'that Alex' had invited him in for a nightcap and he couldn't say no. If he was really late, he would emphasise to her that he couldn't refuse because Alex lived alone and needed the company.

Alex didn't need the company, chose to live alone and resented his circumstances being used as a cover. But if asked, he would lie, not to provide an alibi for Duncan but to protect Ruby. His conscience could accept this as discrete relationships weren't necessarily bad, only sometimes necessary. And he should know this. But he didn't have time for further thought as Duncan handed him a drink.

"Here we go, chaps, chocks away," said Duncan as he took a drink from his own pint glass. Alex wasn't sure where Duncan had picked up some of his vocabulary. He'd been an officer during the war, certainly, and was seen by many as a hero. But it was as if he needed to embellish this and sprinkled his conversation with jargon extracted from the movies, indiscriminately adding RAF patter to his own mess accent. Alex realised he was playing for the audience and wondered, for once, why he needed to do this. Normally, he would have put it down to a means to an end, impress the man and get the business, charm the woman and get her into his bed. But it could be deeper than this, he realised, as if the real Duncan was buried, long ago, deep within his mind and was shackled so that he couldn't escape. His thoughts were interrupted by Fred.

"Alex reckons we're walking again."

"With a bit of luck, old boy. You don't mind, do you?" Although Duncan was smiling, it was clearly a case of 'if you do, tough luck'.

Duncan has once been known to say, when confronted with sleeping with a friend's wife, 'that you could always get new friends but a shag was a shag'. This seemed to pass Fred by and Alex was reminded once again that where emotional matters were concerned Fred was often slow on the uptake.

"No," replied Fred. "But one of these days, you're going to get caught out."

"Faint heart never won fair maid," smiled Duncan.

"In my army, it was faint heart never fucked a pig," laughed Fred. Duncan thought Fred could have a vulgar turn of phrase, picked up from the sergeant's mess and totally unsuitable from him. But it kept him amused and he smiled indulgently.

"Precisely."

Any tension was laughed away and the evening ended in a haze of beer, cigarette smoke and male banter. The Bull was a man's pub, as were most public houses in those days, a retreat from the harsh world and the little woman. Duncan again went to the bar, ostensibly to get more drinks but in reality, to check on his investment. As if swayed by guilt, he bought another round, but this was more to placate his friends and ensure their co-operation. They were laughing as they went out of the bar and into the night.

Duncan, however, remained as men drifted out and the landlord put the stools onto the tables signifying the end of business. He didn't ask Duncan to leave so it was obvious that Alice, the barmaid, had told him he was waiting for her. He also didn't acknowledge him or look him in the eye which made it very clear that he knew Alice was married, didn't approve and wanted no more to do with it. Duncan didn't mind, he preferred married women because they knew the score, wanted a bit of fun the same has he did, weren't generally chasing marriage and if they fell pregnant, well, that's what married women did. No, all in all, he preferred them and they liked him; a bit of charm and excitement from their humdrum world once the gloss had worn off the wedding.

Chapter Eight

"You ready then?" Alice had walked up behind him and linked her arm through his. It was clear that she was not fooled by his intentions and as happy to participate as he was. She was wearing a belted coat and he half noted that, whilst fashionable, it didn't suit her fuller figure. But he'd deal with that later. Laughing, he moved his arm so that she was pulled closer to him and led her outside and up the street to where the Wolseley was parked. He liked the car; it was big and powerful, smelt of leather and wood inside and, more importantly, had a spacious back seat that could accommodate several friends or two discrete adulterers.

"Nice car." She was clearly impressed; at that time, not many people owned cars and this was one of the better ones. She thought it suited him, expensive but not flash, classy.

"Big bugger, isn't it."

"Conveniently so." She picked up his message and smiled. There was no shyness with this one and she liked his confidence. She was used to all the ditherers who came to the bar, men who obviously wanted her but hadn't the bottle to ask or spent hours on the niceties that would get them nowhere. This one knew what he wanted, knew that women wanted him and didn't give a damn if they knew that he knew it. And he also didn't seem to give a damn so that if a woman tried to make him run around, he'd merely walk away. He made the woman do all the running and so they did. Alice didn't know if she liked this but knew she had no choice if she wanted him. And she did.

It was later, as they were parked in a dark lane, stretched in the back of the car, that she realised how much she'd wanted him. Alice was no innocent, and besides her husband, there had been several other men since her marriage, more out of fun and boredom than sexual repression, but now she knew what she'd been missing. She'd had orgasms before, often induced as the men thrust towards their own release, but this was the first time she had been slowly and deliberately driven to one by a man who seemed to take delight in tormenting her, slowly building a response in her until she could no longer breathe and her release came in shudders and waves of pleasure. Only then had he hastened, building speed slowly until his breath quickened and she found herself panting again so that when he came, she felt another orgasm take her. Now, she lay flushed and sweaty as he disentangled himself and adjusted his clothing.

"You okay?" he asked as he slid out of the back seat and into the front driver's seat. It was less of a question, as he already knew the answer to that, and more a conclusion to what had happened. He was finished with her for the time being and wanted rid of her. But he also had to be nice as there would be a few more trysts before he got rid of her. "We'd better get you home to that husband of yours. Don't want him suspecting anything."

"You're okay. I usually walk home so if you just drop me at the end of my street, he'll be no wiser." Alice knew he wanted rid of her and resented it. But she wanted him again so didn't push it. Instead, she got in the front seat and directed him through the maze of terraced housing that formed the old city. On her instruction, he stopped under a lamppost that illuminated the drizzle falling from the dark sky and waited as she opened the door and turned to him. With a brief 'see you later', she quickly pecked him on the cheek and trotted down the street. Watching her retreating back, Duncan was reminded of Mary; she had the same kind of walk that was really a brisk trot on clattering heels. He wondered if there was a barmaid school somewhere that taught them to do it. Slipping into gear he turned the car and headed back through the town.

As he was driving, he mused over his memories of Mary. It was probably because Alice was similar that he'd made the play for her. Contrary to what Alex and Fred thought, he wasn't always on the lookout for women and had been quite content having a few drinks. Also, unbeknownst to them, he was having a fling with the wife of one of his colleagues and that, together with Ruby, was taking both his time and energy. But the resemblance had been strong and he'd wanted her. But he'd wanted rid of Alice when he'd finished, which hadn't been the case with Mary. That had been a bit of madness. He smiled at the thought as he no longer felt any bitterness. In fact, Duncan felt very little; he didn't allow himself anger and the only joy he took was purely physical.

Mary. How he'd fallen for her, drooling like an idiot when he'd gone to the bar with Alex and seen her for the first time. Sitting there, longing for her and not knowing what to do. He'd gone back night and after night just to look at her as he was too tongue-tied to say anything. At first, she'd been amused by the shy youth who gazed at her so adoringly but couldn't speak but this had given way, after his constant visits, to be being flattered by his total infatuation.

One night, she'd fortunately decided to take matters in hand and promptly asked him at closing time if he was going to walk her home. He'd been unable to answer her but had waited patiently by the door, taking her proffered hand nervously as they headed down the lane. He was totally innocent at that time and was content, no delirious, to just hold her hand, feel her lean against him and smell her skin, part perfume, part makeup and, faintly, sweat. He never then, or later, complained of any muskiness on women as he always thought of it as part of the essential being of a woman.

If Duncan had been content to play the courting couple, Mary hadn't and had taken matters in hand. They couldn't go back to his rooms in college and her lodgings didn't allow visitors but it was a warm summer and she was inventive. For the next few weeks, they made use of the balmy nights in hidden corners and shaded spots on the riverbank as she introduced him to the delights that could be offered. She was a good teacher and he an apt pupil as he learnt the art of giving pleasure whilst taking his. But as his enthusiasm for her grew, hers for him seemed to wane. Far from being eager to see him, she seemed full of excuses not to. In desperation, he'd visited her lodgings and, unable to go in, loitered in a nearby alley, settled to await her appearance. But he wasn't prepared when she finally appeared and was met by a tall man in uniform, kissing him in greeting and linking arms as they walked away. It wasn't the kind of kiss you gave a relative and he was left in no doubt that this was more than a passing acquaintance.

He'd quickly overcome the desire to chase after and confront them, he'd been cuckolded and had no wish to be humiliated as well. Besides, if he didn't know about the young officer then he was sure that he didn't know about him. But the hurt persisted and he retreated to a pub near college, taking his drink to a dark corner where he slowly and deliberately had got drunk. He'd followed this pattern for several days until Alex caught up with him, aghast at the dishevelled and unwashed man reeking of drink before him. One look had told Alex that he wouldn't get much sense from him and he'd half dragged, half carried him back to his rooms, walking quickly past the porters to avoid any questions. He'd found out Duncan had gone missing from several of his friends and knew his tutor would have alerted them. Somehow, he'd managed to evade any questions and wrestled him into his rooms and onto the bed. Duncan had instantly fallen into a drunken stupor and Alex had taken the time to brew strong coffee.

Over the next several hours, the sorry incident was related whilst Alex tried in vain to console him. He tried the old trusted route of making light, that he'd had his fun and now it was time to move on. When this didn't work, he'd tried sympathy but this had no effect either. Finally, he got angry and this seemed to work. The one thing Duncan couldn't take was being thought of as a fool. Alex had been relieved and had assumed that here the matter would end. He knew Duncan would mope but eventually come out of his depression a wiser man. Hell, if he thought about it, he may come to remember the episode as a favourable one when he'd become a man.

But Alex was only half right in his view that Duncan would forget Mary and move on. On the surface, he seemed to forget all about her. He even became more outgoing, doing less studying and more drinking with his fellow students who welcomed the change with enthusiasm. He started to become popular and began learning how to foster this new persona, enjoying whatever life threw at him. But if he became more outgoing and popular in a crowd, his emotions were in turmoil and he started to develop the hard-outer shell that would so dominate his later life.

Another nail in his souls' coffin was hammered down a couple of months later when he'd accidentally ran into Mary, having given up the Turf. She'd obviously not heard that he'd seen her soldier boyfriend and assumed he had got the message she wished to cool the relationship. But now she seemed eager to rekindle it and Duncan had simply accepted that. But that was where the old Duncan ended and the new Duncan began.

Whereas before he had been infatuated and the sex had been a bonus and a delight, it was now the only benefit of the relationship. But the more he seemed to care less; the more Mary seemed attracted to him. It ended finally after a liaison in which she'd accused him of coldly using her and he'd agreed and walked off. He'd heard later that the boyfriend had died at Dunkirk, his army service ending before his had even begun. But it never occurred to him that she may have been seeking comfort, he was aware of her desire but not her need. There would be little recognition of such in the future.

The future, however, was rushing forward to meet all of them. There was now a war and life, as they knew it, had stopped. The certainties of life, pummelled by the last war, now submitted themselves to the archives of history as the nation began mobilising to meet a precarious future. Duncan, already losing interest in his studies, joined up and was commissioned to a new battalion of his father's old northern regiment. But for him, there was no immediate action following the debacle of Dunkirk and the phoney war began.

Following three weeks intensive training, the regiment was considered fit for higher training and took part in many Brigade and Divisional exercises in which they excelled. It made no difference and the battalion became operational erecting beach defences. But the weather was fine and generally a good time was had by all. Duncan enjoyed this, joking with the men and mixing more freely than at any other time in his life. But he formed no close attachments, happy to be in a group sharing fun but never engaging in a personal conversation. But this suited the temperament of the others and his popularity rose.

After this time under canvass, the battalion moved further along the south coast and into barracks where they honed their skills in spit and polish, polishing floors and carrying out the essential task of whitewashing the coal buckets. But despite this morale, remained high and the troops enjoyed wandering through the winding streets of the old Kent towns. But, following more beach duties, the real war loomed and on Christmas day 1942, the battalion found itself embarking onto troop ships at Liverpool docks. Duncan would find his life turned around even further than he could imagine.

Chapter Nine

As Duncan was awaiting his embarkation, Ruby was looking forward to her military career. She finally joined the ATS in January 1943 at the age of twenty-one and was posted to London as a clerk. For other provincial girls, being away from home was daunting but Ruby was happy to be away from the confines of her childhood. Not that she was looking for partying or wild times. She had the looks, being of medium height and slender figure accented with curves in the right places. Dark wavy hair complimented pale skin which emphasised the large dark eyes that were her best feature. But the eyes were stern, showing no hint of merriment and intimidating any man brave enough to look into them.

This was a serious girl who took no nonsense and excelled at her work, conscientious and meticulous, accurate and efficient. All officers welcomed her into their commands, an asset that would improve the running of their offices and free up their own time because Ruby was always willing to take on extra work at a level beyond her authority. But if she did this, she was the master, despite the military organisation, of her own life.

There was a great deal of speculation about her background, what could have created such a stern countenance. It had come to light she was from the industrial north and her colleagues envisaged dark satanic mills looming over soot stained terraces dripping with rain and children running ragged in the street. But whereas her childhood knew poverty and was gloomy, the poverty was gentile and the gloom emotional.

She'd started life as a happy child who worshipped her war hero father whom she'd do anything to please, the original daddy's girl. He'd practically raised her during his long spells at home with illness whilst his wife did her best to supplement his meagre income. But her beloved father had finally succumbed to the mustard gas that had crippled his lungs whilst she was still a small child and the centre of her universe disappeared.

Ruby didn't turn taciturn overnight. She was still very young, had the child's capacity to love and craved affection. But the more she craved affection the more her mother withdrew, her sadness turning to despair, despair turning to bitterness and finally, a reserve that was cold and unassailable. Like many others, her mother now took comfort in the Church, not the comfort of love but the cold certainties it seemed to provide. It had rules that gave shape, if not warmth, and a reassurance that whatever her circumstances, she was in the right and entitled to look down on others.

She followed this perverse snobbery by attending the cold and forbidding church whose stone exterior made it imposing but cruel and whose iron railings were reminiscent of a prison. Ruby was dragged to this mausoleum every Sunday and grew to hate its interior that was dank and always seemed to have dust hanging in the air, carrying with it a musty smell as it blocked the nostrils. This was no joyous place to praise the lord, but a stern institution to rule the mind and body.

The church was presided over by the Reverend Tomkins whose shabby and shapeless black suit hung from a cadaverous body making him the epitome of the building he served. His cold clammy hand matched his black, greasy hair and his overall countenance seemed reminiscent of a crow. His wife was no more attractive, with an out of date cloche hat pulled hard down over her angular features accentuating their sharpness and creating a brooding air that terrified children. It was just as well they didn't have any although nobody of their acquaintance could imagine them being intimate enough to produce them.

The reverend tended to his diminishing flock whilst his wife maintained a cold house and an even more miserable women's guild. The women who attended did so out of a perceived need for socially respectability, or occasionally to escape an even worse husband, so that the group provided little emotional support and a great deal of bitter criticism. The one person who seemed to flourish in this atmosphere was Ruby's mother who felt badly used by the world at large and was willing, even secretly happy, to observe the miseries of greater sinners.

Ruby was plunged deeper into this emotional void as her mother became increasingly attached to the church in general and Mrs Tomkins in particular. They made an incongruous pair who gained from each other's company but cared not a jot for their welfare. Ruby was dragged along but took no part in their activities, learning to keep in the background. To be seen and not heard and give no cause for concern. The sunny child disappeared, she received care but not outward affection at home and was discouraged from forming bonds with other girls her age whom her mother thought unsuitable. But Ruby was resourceful and tenacious. She knew she had to escape and that the only person who could help was herself. So, she threw herself into her school work, climbing to the top of her class over the years gaining the admiration of her teachers and envy of her fellow pupils. But she had no distractions with friends being discouraged and no conflicting ambitions. Hers was to simply leave.

Admiration came later from a more unlikely source. As she reached puberty and her studies began to take on a more mature aspect, the Reverend Tomkins began to take an interest. His offer to help supervise her homework was readily accepted by her mother if not as eagerly greeted by herself. Until then she had only viewed the Reverend as a cold distant figure who delivered his dry sermons on a Sunday but otherwise ignored her. This had suited her admirably and she now found his attentions both irritating and frightening. At first, he was coldly professional, checking her syllabus and commenting on her reading. But as time went by, and Ruby developed into a pretty young woman, his attentions became more familiar. He found more and more time to spend in her company and she would look up to see him watching her. Always watching, but never speaking, she felt his attentions becoming more and more disturbing. Through all this, nothing untoward happened although the anticipation that something could was even more intimidating. She was just getting used to, if not comfortable with, his brooding presence when the situation changed.

It was on a particularly damp Wednesday in March that showed none of the promise of spring and the few trees stood forlornly against a darkening sky that she let herself into the manse and made her way to the study to start her homework. Normally, he would appear after she had begun but to her surprise, he was waiting for her. More to her surprise was the fact that a fire burned in the grate. The reverend was as parsimonious as he was a parson and believed that cold kept the mind alert.

"I thought it was such a miserable day that a little fire would raise the atmosphere whilst we worked," he stated by way of explanation.

"That's most generous of you," Ruby had replied, although she wondered what he really wanted. This became crystal clear when he's leaned across to look at her work and stroked her hair.

"You're a very pretty girl." Her whole body recoiled from his touch and she backed away from him but he followed her until she was trapped in a corner. "Don't be like that," he'd chided as he leant forward to kiss her.

Without knowing how, she gathered enough strength to push him away and escape though the door. He pursued her but she outran him, out of the door and along the street whereas he stopped at the door as if realising his mistake and not wishing to make a scene in public. Her feet didn't stop until she'd reached home and was just about to enter the house.

At this point, she'd stopped to catch her breath and work out what to tell her mother. She'd realised, at this point, that her mother would probably not believe her as she believed the reverend could do no wrong. She would come to the conclusion that either Ruby was mistaken or, worse, that she had made it the story up. There would be questions about whether she had encouraged him and comments about the dangers of flirting. Whatever happened, Tomkins would be believed innocent and she would be branded neurotic or a liar. She would have to keep things to herself for the time being. *As usual*, she thought.

She did not, however, have to wait long to resolve the matter. As she opened the door, she'd found her mother in front of the hall mirror, adjusting her hat and scarf.

"You're back early," she said as she buttoned her coat and turned. "I was just going to see the minister's wife and thought I'd have a word with him before I walked back with you." She looked at her critically and frowned. "And where's your coat?" Ruby realised that in her rush to escape, she had left everything at the manse. She thought fast.

"I just needed a book, I thought I could run back quickly for it."

"Well, go get it and we'll walk back together. It's not like you to be this silly." Ruby vanished and picked up the first book she came across. As they walked along the street, she decided on her further course of action. She would enter the manse with her mother in sight of the reverend so that he knew she was not alone and therefore not in a position to be trapped. She would then let her mother go and see Mrs Tomkins whilst she went into the study. She knew that the Reverend would follow her and would also be worried by the presence of her mother and that she was talking to his wife. Ruby knew she had to play on that fear and the fact that she knew what the outcome of a wider knowledge of the incident would be. In all probability, she would be disbelieved, but she had to play on his doubts about that. It dawned on her that she could actually gain from the situation.

Ruby shortly found herself at the forbidding manse. As she had expected, the Reverend was lurking in the hallway as they arrived and came forward to look anxiously at her mother's face. Her mother was unaware of this but Ruby observed every expression on his face, from the fear of confrontation to the confusion nothing seemed amiss to the disbelief that he might be going to get away with his indiscretion. It was at this point that Ruby started using her trump card.

Looking towards her mother, she simply said, "You go have your chat with Mrs Tomkins. I'll be in the study when you've finished." She'd chosen her words carefully so as not to arouse suspicion in her mother whilst raising it in Tomkins. Her mother nodded her head and turned as Ruby went back into the room.

Ruby was barely halfway across the room when the door closed behind her and she turned around to face him. He hadn't expected that and stopped abruptly in the middle of the room. She looked him straight in the eye which shook him and stopped any action he might have considered taking.

"One word from you and I'll start screaming," she heard herself saying. "Mother isn't that far away."

"Don't be hasty," he placated, "I only wanted to talk about our little misunderstanding." He was clearly on the back foot and Ruby realised that the battle was half won. She realised he hadn't expected her to fight him and run but rather to sit, even if terrified, whilst he did what he wanted. Now he had lost control and the uncertainty strengthened her resolve.

"There was no misunderstanding, you knew exactly what you were doing and so do I. What do you think your congregation are going to think?"

"They won't believe it." His answer was quick but she detected the doubt, and more importantly fear, in his response.

"Whether they believe it or not, you won't be trusted again. Your wife won't be able to hold her head up and I'll bet she'll make it uncomfortable for you." Her words were hitting home and she could see him flinch.

"What do you want to do?" His tone was cold, but wary.

"I'll tell you. I want nothing more to do with here. You've been saying how you could get me a scholarship through the church. You do that and I'll leave and that will be the end of it."

"And what about when you come back?"

"Oh, I won't be coming back." And she never did.

Chapter Ten

By January 1943, Duncan had landed in North Africa. His ship had approached Algiers in the early hours and he had stood entranced as the sun came up and bathed the coast from amber to green and the warmth hit him. It was the first, and last, time he saw any beauty in the country.

Algiers was in chaos as they disembarked. Military vehicles were driving across the docks kicking up clouds of dust as netting emerged from the ships holds carrying equipment and supplies. Everywhere were the Arabs, dressed in rags and waiting to steal anything they could. It was hot, dry, dusty and smelly and nothing like the Kasbah from fiction or in the movies. From this melee, the battalion was, at last, formed up and began the long-forced march to their designated camp.

This was twenty miles away and, unused to the heat and after confinement on the ship, the men became strung out and arrived in late evening. Amidst a sea of tents that formed the camp the men settled down for the night. In the balmy evening, the men shed their clothes only to find that the temperature dropped to freezing during the night and they woke as shivering wrecks. As the sun rose, the heat returned and bodies once frozen were again bathed in sweat. Duncan had moved through his men aware of their mutterings as he went.

Duncan's phony war was over and his real one was beginning. Before, he had been running from himself, becoming the brash bonhomie and keeping his feelings to himself. Now he was confronted with the harsh realities as battle began. Before, it was about marching and training but now the fighting began in earnest and he saw his muttering men begin to die. The regiment had originally been formed as skirmishers and had a reputation as front line troops.

They, thus, found themselves in the thick of the fighting. Duncan had known that men would die but was unprepared for the sheer brutality in which they died. Blown apart by mortar shell and artillery, mowed down by machine gun and dying in hand to hand combat all glory was forgotten in the gore that followed. Things came to a head when, just short of Tunis, at Long Stop, he saw his friend Stephen, a fellow Oxford man and officer, destroyed by an artillery shell.

One minute he was there, the next there was just a pile of dirty red earth where he'd been. A charming man with a bright future he was no more in an instant. Another part of Duncan died there and fatalism began to take hold. He never lost his charm but the shell he had created for himself finally sealed in the boy he had been and it was a different man who landed in Sicily. As part of operation Husky, Duncan and the regiment drove the Germans out of the Island in what Churchill described as the soft underbelly of Europe. Here the fighting was lighter than expected, as Hitler had been duped of the Allies intent and left only two battalions to defend the island and Duncan began to relax. There was no final battle in Messina either, as the cornered troops had been evacuated. As a consequence, the advance against the Italian mainland in September would take more time and cost the Allies more troops than they anticipated and change Duncan's life more than he had anticipated.

Chapter Eleven

As the Allied invasion was underway and Duncan found himself fighting ever northwards, a newly commissioned Ruby was posted to Naples as a section officer. Here her duties mirrored what she been doing in London unpaid and unauthorised. The dark and glamorous task of overseeing leave requests and arranging travel warrants.

Sitting at her desk, one day, she was disturbed as a young officer entered the room. Looking up, she was instantly taken by how much he reminded her of her beloved father, the same impish grin, relaxed gait and the charm that tangibly exuded from him. There were even a physical resemblance, same height, build and ascetic features. For once, the stern exterior wavered as she asked what she could do for him.

"Lots actually," he replied. "But first, are you the lovely person I need to see about a furlough?" Her head immediately informed her that here was a charmer who should be avoided, but her heart intervened.

"What else do you want?" she asked simultaneously regretting the invitation whilst looking forward to the response.

"A guide would be useful. I don't have much time and company is always appreciated." This was said with a grin and despite herself, she nodded agreement. "What time do you finish here?" he added.

"Shortly," she replied.

"Good, I'll wait for you." Again, she nodded agreement much to the amazement of Ivy, newly arrived from England who Ruby had taken under her wing and warned against the intentions of young officers.

And so, it was that a short time later, Ruby found herself sitting outside a small Trattoria overlooking a Plaza with a glass of red wine. The city had suffered during the war but with the influx of thousands of allied troops and a flourishing black market, the small restaurants had managed to stay open and welcome the invaders.

My lucks in, thought Duncan, *a new city, a furlough and a pretty girl.* Duncan was in no doubt she was pretty and petite enough to suit his tastes. But his instincts told him this was not a girl to mess with. She was steely, determined with no frivolity. He was frankly amazed she'd agreed to come with him so quickly.

His amazement was nothing compared to Ruby's. She broken every one of her own rules and was aware of Ivy's look as she had left the office. But there was something about Duncan that had captivated her. It wasn't just his similarity to her father; although that had shaken her, but it was that she sensed in him a vulnerability akin to her own. Whereas she covered hers with steel, he masked his with camaraderie and a devil may care attitude, a seeker of pleasure living by his senses. But she was attracted to him, wanted to be with and care for him.

Duncan was not feeling anything similar but found he enjoyed her company. It was clear to him that she wouldn't be an easy conquest but he found that he wasn't bothered by that. It was quite pleasant not having to put on the charm and to relax and be himself. In a way, it helped him reach back to the boy he'd been, when he'd been serious and desperate for someone to love him. It hadn't been any kind of revelation when he'd discovered he was attractive to women, more that he'd given up caring what they thought and had pursued what he'd wanted with a charm offensive that worked.

If he'd been able to stand back and consider this, he might have been a different person, more content and sure of himself, but the game was needed as a constant boost to his confidence so that he pursued women even when his physical interest was minimal. It was as if couldn't help himself. But this girl threw him, he wanted her but didn't need the charm to get her interest. If he'd been a bit more perceptive, he'd have realised that is previous encounters had been shallow and physical but for a man who loved women he didn't know them at all.

"Where do you come from?" The question was another novelty for him, normally he couldn't have cared less about a woman's background unless as a lever to get her in his bed, but he found he was genuinely interested. Ruby, on the other hand, was taken aback, her past was a secret that was sacrosanct and not to be delved into.

"The north," she replied, not tartly but as if that was all the explanation that was needed and no more would be forthcoming.

"That's a pretty big area. Can you be more specific?"

"Not really, it was a big ugly place with nothing much going for it and I have no intention of going back so the question is irrelevant."

"You have no family there?"

"None that I care to see." Duncan realised there was no point in pursuing the subject. It was also clear to him that here was another person who, like him, was adrift in the world, and for whom, like himself, the war and the army had offered a refuge. He thought to change the subject.

"What would you like to eat?"

"Whatever is on the menu?" It was a good answer; the food locally was good simple and cheap but you took what you could get. So, they finished up eating pasta washed down with red wine on the first of many nights which were to follow a similar pattern until Duncan received his next posting.

Chapter Twelve

Life changed suddenly for Duncan in Lauro in northern Italy in early 1944. During the offensive to evict the last of the German forces, he and his unit came under a heavy barrage from the enemy and his luck finally ran out. One moment he was sat in a dug out and the next, he was being thrown in the air. He was luckier than many of his men for whom the war, and life, ended that day in the mud and sludge the guns churned up. He himself escaped with concussion, mild shell shock and a shrapnel would in his leg that left him with a slight limp that remained with him for the rest of his life. Being Duncan, he later embellished tales of how he'd received this wound and, together with his roguish charm, this only added to the debonair façade he created. But in a more crucial way, it set the course which the rest of his life would follow.

The wounds sustained were sufficient for him to escape the front and be transferred to the military hospital in Caserta in the south near Naples and, more importantly, near Ruby. She had seen his name on the list of casualties that arrived at the office and had headed immediately to the hospital after she had discovered his destination. Here she had found a very different Duncan from the brash young officer who had so beguiled her.

Confined to a bed in military blue pyjamas, with his leg dressed and suspended, he presented a very subdued persona. This was compounded by the fact that he was in a long dormitory ward with about fifty other patients, many of whom were shell shocked and heavily sedated, adding to the depressive atmosphere. Duncan himself was still suffering from mild shock following the explosion that had sailed him across the field and this, together with his incapacity, caused the vulnerability he had suppressed for years to resurface. He found he needed someone and Ruby provided that comfort.

Her attachment to him grew and her need to protect him, if only from himself. It began a strange courtship based on his vulnerability and her need to express love. This was not a relationship based on passion, no coup de foudre occurred, yet something deeper was developing. He was the only man she would ever love and the only man she would ever sleep with. He later told her, when asked, that she was the only woman he had ever loved and that he had never loved his other girlfriends.

She began visiting daily, if her duties permitted, at first sitting by his bed holding his hand, talking in hushed tones about his background, being amazed by his underlying intellect. They later progressed to sitting outside in the sunshine where she could bring him little treats to bolster the army food, sipping coffee and eating whatever cakes she could find. As his strength returned, she would walk with him around the grounds, supporting him and chiding him for his impatience even though he was making a good recovery.

However, it was not quick enough for him to return to his battalion. With the Germans finally ousted, it had moved on and with his disabilities he was destined to finish his service in an administrative role in Italy. Not that he objected very much, the work was not only safe but very easy, Italy was beautiful and he had time to explore and rekindle his love affair with the renaissance and stimulate the intellect he had left dormant for so long. This was the other side of Duncan, the unseen and deeper psyche he kept from others and, quite often, himself. But Ruby was now invited into that world, accompanying him on his tourist jaunts, fascinated by his depth of knowledge and his willingness to share himself.

Where he became more open and vulnerable, she became more protective and possessive, and this possession led to the inevitable, one night in a small pension near to the ancient site of Pompeii. They had booked separate rooms, as they had become accustomed to do, next to each other. Duncan had never pushed for a double room because he never saw Ruby as one of his conquests; she was someone who'd been there when he needed her, who had held his hand when he knew fear and had guided his steps as he'd recovered.

He was somewhat surprised, therefore when, after they had retired, his door had creaked open and she had slid into bed beside him. He was even more surprised when he realised that although she knew what she wanted; she had no idea how to go about it. It was a new experience for him, the virginal he had never pursued, and his women had all known the pleasure they wanted.

He found himself being uncharacteristically gentle, less concerned with providing physical pleasure and more concerned with displaying tenderness. This was exactly what Ruby wanted, to cement their relationship and know that he was hers. For him, it was a new kind of lovemaking, not driven by lust or urgency but more a comfortable and reassuring intimacy. It established a pattern where the lovemaking, if not frequent, was regular enough to maintain their intimacy.

How long this situation would have continued became academic as Duncan, because of his wounds, became eligible for early demobilisation. Ruby, despite his comforting, was distraught. Having given herself so completely, she could only see the chasm opening before her that his absence would create. They had sat all night working over the problem, drinking endless coffees and brandies, smothering her tears until a solution had been reached.

Duncan had never thought about what he was going to do after the war; he had enlisted following his disastrous affair with Mary and lived day by day during his service. But his love of academia had been reawakened by his sojourn in Italy and they decided he should return to college and complete his studies. Ruby, on her demobilisation, would join him and they would then decide where their future was. Neither had any ties but to each other and the horizons were open.

Strangely, marriage was never mentioned though it never occurred to either of them that they wouldn't be together. The day finally arrived for his departure and it was a scene reminiscent of that witnessed at the start of the war by many people as they parted at the station as he boarded the train that would take him through Italy and Switzerland, along to Calais and finally back to England.

Chapter Thirteen

It was a warm day when Duncan found himself back in Oxford. The unchanging streets and spires spoke of the past but, whilst he revelled in the feeling of euphoria, it was a very different Duncan who had returned. Gone was the naïve boy and a mature battle-hardened man stood in his place. He no longer caught the scowl of college porters but more a respectful nod as he passed through the gates. What he did find the same was his love of books and the smell of the library and the joy of study. His affection for Italy, the classics and specifically, the renaissance grew and was a reminder of Ruby but as time passed the memory of her merged into the abstract remembrance of the place and the moments, they had shared faded.

He was, in fact, revelling in his renewed freedom no longer fettered by duty to the army, his disability and her ministrations. In truth, he missed her but he had always been self-contained and their time together had been the exception to this. To some, absence made the heart grow fonder but, in his case, although he had fond memories and feelings for her, he was not tied by enduring loyalty. And yet it was by accident that his infidelity began.

As he was walking through town one day, he heard his name called and turned to see a figure waving to him. It took a moment before he realised it was Mary; the war years had not been kind to her and she was holding a child's hand. He remembered that she had married a soldier who had been killed and assumed the child, a small boy, was his. Other men would have thought that he could have been his if circumstances had been different but the thought never crossed his mind. He was looking at Mary, noting that she was thicker around the waist, her face was worn and there were wrinkles around her eyes. Her body appeared weary.

"Hello, Duncan, how are you?" Even her voice was tired and he wondered what had happened to the vivacious girl he had known who was full of life and fun. It was what had attracted him to her, she had been the opposite of him at the time and what he wanted to be. But now the tables had turned and there was nothing there. For all his hedonism, Duncan wasn't, and would never become, malicious and he took no delight in her fall. To an extent, he felt sorry for her but that was all he felt for her. There was no affection remaining and certainly no attraction.

"I'm okay. How are you?" He didn't offer any further information and only asked out of ingrained politeness. To be honest, he didn't really care how she felt and had no curiosity.

"Not too bad. It's not easy raising a child on your own. My husband was killed early in the war." She smiled sadly and yet looked at him somewhat eagerly at the same time. An invitation perhaps and an opportunity for him to pick up where they had left off. But as she looked, she saw the disinterest in his eyes. She no longer attracted him. He was no longer the callow youth desperate for love and her flaws were now apparent to him.

"I'm sorry about that. We lost a lot of good people." The response was what you would give to a stranger and the hurt clearly showed in her eyes. "Well, I'd better dash," he said excusing himself. Turning, he walked away without looking back and that was the last time he saw her.

"An old friend," said a voice next to him. He turned and saw Jane, the wife of one of the college tutors, standing by the side of the street. In her early forties, she was an attractive woman with a knowing smile.

"Something like that," he replied, straightening up and looking her in the eye. "She's someone I knew from before the war."

"I thought she must be. She doesn't appear to be your type."

"Oh, and what is my type?" She was playing with him but he was enjoying the game. It was a long time since he'd played it but the old instincts were still there.

"That would be telling," she laughed. "But where are you heading?"

"I was going to the library but that can wait. I feel that I need a drink. I could also use some company. Care to join me?"

"What, me a married woman, and in Oxford. What can you be thinking?" But even as she said it, he knew she would. The chase was on and he knew he'd already won.

"You'd be doing me a favour," he said smiling.

"Oh, all right then, but it had better be somewhere respectable." With that they headed to a small hotel off Broad Street where people were having afternoon tea and found a quiet corner where they could enjoy an early gin and tonic. It was just as well they'd gone to a hotel thought Duncan as he lay in bed on his back smoking a cigarette later on. Jane lay against him under his arm, her free hand stroking his chest. He'd booked the room after a couple of drinks and they'd gone up quietly and separately.

Once inside the room, all pretence had been forgotten and what had followed could only be described as gratuitous sex on both parts. It contained no romance or love just physical need. Jane had been demanding but underlying that he sensed she needed to be wanted, to be desired. That had suited him fine; he desired her but didn't want any attachment beyond that.

"What time do you need to be back and what will you tell him?" Duncan was already covering his tracks. He knew her husband; who was a lecturer in the same college, and wanted to get their stories straight.

"As long as I'm back for dinner, it will be okay. I don't think he'd notice I was missing otherwise." There was a hint of bitterness in her voice and Duncan quickly picked up what the situation was. He knew her husband and thought him not a bad chap. But he was a lot older than her and completely immersed in his work, the traditional academic. He sensed that she felt neglected, was lonely and craved both attention and physical release. If she was needy that was fine but he would be careful not to let an emotional attachment develop.

Duncan had several more liaisons with Jane during which he let slip that he had a girlfriend called Ruby who would be joining him when she could. Jane couldn't argue because she was a married woman with a husband she wasn't going to leave. Inevitably, the passion cooled and the affair fizzled out. But it opened Duncan's eyes to other opportunities. The university was full of women who had married older men who had impressed them with their intellect but later disappointed them with their lack of attention. Duncan was always there to offer consolation and take advantage of their loneliness and needs. As his studies progressed, he cut a swathe through the ranks of neglected wives, careful not to become emotionally entangled.

Chapter Fourteen

Fred lay looking down the barrel of his rifle wishing for the first time for rain. Having endured several monsoon seasons and the disease and misery they brought; he'd never thought he'd be glad to see it again. But the smell wafting towards him was becoming unbearable and only water could wash it away. The Japanese, in their quest to capture Imphal, had got their tactics completely wrong and insanely driven their sick and starving troops to attack in droves to be mown down like wheat. In the intense heat, hundreds of bodies lay broken on the ground. Unrecovered, they became bloated and burst adding noxious fumes to the nightmare tableau. Fred thought he was used to such horrors but it sickened even him. It was a far cry from his journey out to Burma and he was far from the boy he was.

When he signed up, he was still a boy, just of age and wanting to be involved before his call up. Puffing up his chest and squaring his shoulders, he'd marched into the recruiting office, the epitome of the boys in the previous war who tried to look stern and had grown wispy moustaches in an attempt to look older. Like them he was full of enthusiasm but he was unlike his fellows who were conscripts and openly fearful. Many were from the docklands and had experienced intensive bombing and seen horrors first hand whereas he, in the suburbs, and his comfortable school, had only been subject to patriotic press reports and the gossip of his parents' friends of the heroics of their offspring.

He'd found the barracks and early training hard at first but his enthusiasm, good nature and willingness to try anything and help others had endeared him to his fellows and his fitness, which was to serve him well later, made the life of his trainers easier and kept him out of trouble. His education and intelligence should have picked him out for officer training but his youth held him back. Besides, he was the baby of the troop and wanted to stay with the men.

The men, in many ways, adopted him and he became something of a company mascot. When he tried too hard, they would hold him back and when someone tried to take advantage of his good nature, they were quick to intervene. He was a boy and they looked after him like older brothers and saw to his development as a man. In their view, this involved taking him into the man's world of the bar.

He'd never really had a drink before. His father liked to go out but he had always been too young to go with him and his mother would have disapproved. He was her baby and she wanted him to remain so. There had been terrible rows when he'd informed them he wanted to join the army instead of going to teacher training as she'd wanted him to do. His father didn't want him to go either. He'd been in the first war and still suffered from the effects. But he saw the boy's enthusiasm and didn't want to reject or embarrass him.

In the end, they'd reached a compromise: he would take a temporary job as a clerk until he was old enough to enlist. His father had placated his mother by the hope that by the time that happened, the war would probably be over, and if it wasn't, he would have been drafted anyway. So, he had reluctantly gone to the office of a solicitor his father knew until the time arrived. When it did, he had a tearful farewell with his mother and a manly handshake from his father and boarded his train.

But he was in the army and trying hard to be a man. He went out with the rest of his squad to a local pub popular with the men.

"What do you want, young un?" shouted Smith, known as Smudger, as he battled through the throng.

Not knowing what to order, Fred took the easy option, "I'll have the same as you."

"Good man," laughed Smudger and passed a pint to him. Fred had never drank beer before, his father liked one before Sunday lunch but it was never kept in the house as he preferred whisky. Up until now, his experience of alcohol had been confined to a Christmas sherry. Bravely, he took a long swallow and was surprised both by its slightly bitter taste and smooth fullness. He decided he liked it and took another long swallow.

"Careful, boy, you're not used it," said Smudger putting his arm protectively around his shoulder.

"I can handle it," Fred replied, "and anyway it's my round." His father had drilled into him that a man stood his round and was beholding to no one. And he desperately wanted to be a man. He got more beers from the bar. As he drank his second, the first began to take effect. But instead of feeling sick, he felt a warm glow and a sense of ease. He also felt confident and ready to take on the world.

"Okay, boy, it's time to make you a man. It's your first time out, I guess so you're supposed to only have one beer and shag three women." The other man laughed at the joke. But Fred was feeling happy enough to be cocky.

"Can't I have three beers and shag one woman!" The others laughed even louder. Fred revelled in the laughter not really comprehending what he had said.

"Okay," said Smudger, "someone get the drinks in. The rest of you get your hands in your pockets." The men started dropping coins into Smudger's cap.

Drinks were bought, and consumed, and a happy Fred was steered from the pub by Smudger.

"Where are we going?" he asked.

"You'll see," laughed Smudger, his arm around his shoulder as he steered him through the narrow-terraced streets and down towards the docks. Fred didn't really see where he was going, he was happily drunk and enjoying the revelry. After a while, they stopped and Fred saw a woman standing in the semi darkness by an alley entry. His mate went across to talk to the woman and he saw their heads close together as they whispered something, looking across to him as they did so. Smudger then gestured for him to join them and he staggered over. His friend was suddenly looking very serious and sober.

"This lady is going to look after you. Go and enjoy. This is on the lads." With that the woman took him by the hand and led him into the dark recesses of the alley. She pulled him close and he could smell the cheap perfume and powder, underlying sweat and cigarette smoke. It would normally have offended him, as would the roughness of her coat but he'd never been that close to a woman and the warmth she was generating.

"Okay, dear," she said as her hands dropped and opened his flies. He didn't know what to do as her fingers explored, but his body reacted automatically. Within a short time, he was ready and soon, still stood, he felt himself entering into the warmth of her. The thought crossed his mind I'm a man now as his body released. And then it was over and he was heading back to his friends.

"Okay, lad, had a good time?" Smudger was smiling again.

"Yes, great. I'm tired now." And with that they headed back to the barracks.

When Fred awoke, he was back in his bed and at first, couldn't remember getting there. Then the previous evening came back to him along with an aching head and tingling along his loins. *I'm a man now,* he thought, having done the deed being more important than any pleasure he'd received from it. In truth, he'd received little, too drunk to enjoy it much and, to be honest, not that bothered. He'd enjoyed the drink, the euphoria it had given him and the camaraderie he'd shared with the lads. He felt himself shaken, *Up and at them, it's time for parade. There's a war on you know.*

The war had, indeed, not ended and Fred soon found himself on a troopship in Liverpool bound for Burma to join what was to become known as the forgotten army charged with fighting the Japanese and preventing the invasion of India. The atmosphere on the ship was quite relaxed after they left the main submarine areas and the weather remained relatively calm. They only had to wear boots every third day to stop their feet becoming soft and a sort of holiday spirit prevailed. There was a lot of banter and Fred came in for a fair share of it as his exploits were described in great detail to the delight of his fellows. Fred didn't mind and revelled in the notoriety. It was also when he acquired his nickname 'the lady killer'. This would be shortened, but that was later.

After a long voyage, they reached their destination in central India. They discovered then that they were to be part of a new force under Orde Wingate acting as a long-range penetration group behind enemy lines. To train them for this Wingate used the jungles at Saugor, near Jansi, preparing them for bivouac life, jungle warfare, river crossings and the care and handling of mules. The new force became known as Chindits, a mispronunciation of the Burmese word 'Chinthe'; the mythical creature that stood guard outside pagodas. The Chindits themselves would become a thing of myth and legend themselves but at great cost. Training conditions were hard and their original equipment was out of date and inadequate. But they muddled through until assignment.

Their first action was supposed to be part of a coordinated push against the enemy but the larger part of the operation was called off. However, Wingate decided to push on with the Chindits; partly to test their ability and also to assess the enemy's strength and disrupt their communications. In what became known as operation Loincloth, three thousand men penetrated deep into enemy territory, Fred and Smudger among them. At first, they were successful, cutting railway lines and launching attacks. The strategy of long-range penetration worked; the force was large enough to mount devastating attacks but small enough to evade capture.

Supplied by air, they further confused the enemy who searched vainly for supply lines in a classical military response. They were over a thousand miles within enemy territory when their luck ran out. Fierce weather conditions and sickness debilitated the force and they were forced to withdraw. The seriously wounded and sick were airlifted out but the rest of the troops had to march back over jungle terrain, crossing rivers whilst being battered by the weather and harassed by the enemy. Vicious hand to hand fighting ensued and Fred fought along with the other men. But the change came midway through the march when they walked into an ambush and were rushed. Smudger shot one opponent but couldn't stop a second. Fred watched in horror as a bayonet was thrust into his friend's stomach and to his dying day would remember the look of surprise on his face and realisation that he had been killed before he crumpled.

As Smudger fell to the ground, Fred leapt forward and hit his killer with his rifle butt. He then employed the old soldier's attack of using the butt in conjunction with the boot until his opponent was dead and mangled. He had carried on until dragged away by his platoon, the other assailants having broken and run. The other soldiers now treated him warily; he was no longer the boy but a man to be feared. They suffered further engagements during the withdrawal where Fred's wildness continued. But, if he made his fellows nervous, he terrified the foe.

He was always in the thick of the fighting, killing as he went and that made the others job easier and earned him a grudging respect. His almost pathological need to protect the men also endeared him, as well as fighting for them he was always there to lend a hand to the stumbling and weary, to heft a pack or pull a man across the water. And this was needed on the arduous withdrawal. Eventually, they managed to reach the relative safety of Imphal but at great loss. But the respite was sure not to last.

But now, as he lay looking down the barrel of his rifle, even he was sickened by the carnage which had finally washed away his blood lust and need for revenge. The enemy, driven forward by their generals, against the directives of high command, were both sick and starving, tired and broken. Still they came forward towards what was to become their biggest defeat of the war. As the dead littered the land, his anger and hatred for them evaporated and the realisation of the stupidity of what was happening came to him. But he was a soldier and he carried on.

Very soon, he was back in the jungle again, forging ahead in the deep penetration units, cutting communication and supply lines as the Japanese were driven back from a counter offensive and the so-called race for Rangoon began. By the time conflict had ended of the three thousand officers and men who originally entered the jungle, only two thousand one hundred and eighty-two returned. Most of them were sick with malnutrition and tropical disease and only six hundred were passed as fit for further active service. During the rest of his life, on the rare occasions when he would talk about it, he often repeated the litany, 'we lost one in every three, did I tell you that?' Fred was one of the luckier ones, he was reassigned and finished his service as a sergeant in a parachute regiment. He left the army without regret but with a scar on his soul that would never heal.

Chapter Fifteen

Fred arrived home with his belongings in a kitbag and his demob suit in a cardboard box tied with string under his arm. The old street looked the same but after Asia, appeared glum in the early spring light. Its appearance wasn't helped by its look of neglect, the once proud houses suffering peeling paintwork and recovering from blacked out and taped windows. The chilly wind blowing further dampened his spirits and deepened his despair. He didn't really know what he was doing there but returning home had been the wish of all the men and the mantra that had maintained them in the bitterest days. But now, to Fred, it seemed futile, nothing could ever be the same again and that made all he had been through seem even more futile.

It wasn't that he was bitter; it would have been better if he had been, then at least he would have comprehended what was wrong. It was more as if he were just numb, nothing enthused him and the bright-eyed optimistic boy no longer existed. He knew he should have been happy but everything seemed pointless. It was with leaden feet that he walked up the path of the neat semi-detached house and knocked on the door; he hadn't told anyone he was coming, not because he wanted to surprise them but more that until that moment, he wasn't sure he was coming. But he couldn't really decide what he wanted and so drifted home.

As he stood, the door was opened by his mother who looked older and more worn, thinner and grey. It wasn't only him on whom the war had had an effect. The annoyance on her face at being disturbed vanished and was replaced by one of astonishment then relief and finally joy. She stepped forward and put her arms around him.

"Why didn't you tell me you were coming? I've got nothing ready. Let me look at you." The words were tumbling out. "Come on, come in, don't stand like a stranger? And why are you knocking?"

It was because he felt like a stranger, but he couldn't tell her that. "I didn't want to give you a shock just walking in."

"And you think this didn't. Silly boy." She led him into the hall. His father, hearing voices, appeared at the head of the stairs. Without hesitation, he came rushing downstairs to grab him. Fred was surprised as his father had never been a demonstrative man.

"Freddy, my boy, let me look at you."

Nobody had called him Freddy since he'd left home and despite himself, he felt the emotion rising. As his father pushed him away to look at him, it gave him the opportunity to look more closely at him. Like his mother, he looked older, which was to be expected, but like her he also looked worn and grey. Fred came back down from the sudden and unexpected elation he had felt. His father had been watching him and saw the change in the moods crossing his face.

"Why didn't you tell us you were coming?"

"I've just asked him that," his mother cut in. "I haven't even got his room ready."

"Don't be silly, woman, you've kept his room like a shrine."

"I haven't even made his bed up." She wasn't to be distracted, and had to be seen to be welcoming. "And I've got to make him something special for dinner."

"Good, you can make me something special too. Come on, son, I was going for a quick pint before dinner, come with me and make your dad proud."

"Is that all right, Mum?"

"Of course, get him out of my way so I can get on. Be back for seven."

The pair of them walked to the end of the street and turned into the High Street. In his youth, the street, with its butchers, grocers, post office and bank had seemed exciting but now it seemed twee, no longer the snow-covered chocolate-box Christmas vision he remembered. Little England was no more but he felt nothing at its passing. In the middle of the street stood the Rose and Crown and they entered the saloon bar.

"What are you having?" his father asked him.

"I'll have a pint please."

"I see you've been getting bad habits while you've been away." Turning to the barman he said, "Two pints, Jack. This is my lad back from Burma."

"Must have been rough, son," said Jack pulling at the pump.

You don't know the half of it, thought Fred. Instead he replied, "It was okay. You do what you have to do."

"Quite right. These are on the house by the way." Muttering their thanks, they took seats near the fire where a small stack of coal burned in the grate. Not the roaring pub fire of the past but welcome as it was a cold day and the place was quiet at that time.

"How was it really, son?" Fred looked up and saw his father looking straight at him. He wasn't sure what to say.

"It was rough to be honest. We lost a lot of people and there was too much killing. At first, I thought that was what we were there for but in the end, it just sickened you. But you still did it." *And I did my share and more,* he thought *and I don't know why.* "In the end, it was so senseless." He looked at his father whose eyes were grave and tired.

"I know what it's like. I was in the last one and we never thought it could happen again. It's senseless but you can't do anything else. It's disgusting and should never happen. There's nothing noble about it no matter what people tell you. Believe me, you never really get over it."

Fred was surprised; his father had never talked about his service before and had frowned at the warmongers in the papers. A lifelong Tory, he hated Churchill for Gallipoli. The only thing Fred remembered from his childhood was how he had looked sadly at the homeless men who had returned and were now hopeless alcoholics. He'd seen him sympathetically give money to some of the maimed who had given all and were now forgotten.

As he thought this, his father observed. "You've finished already. Never mind, you deserve it. I'll get another, just don't tell your mother or she'll have my guts for garters."

I very much doubt it, thought Fred. It was a game his parents had played for as long as he could remember. His father would always pop out for a quick one which invariably meant two. He would give a time and rush in twenty minutes late full of apologies. His mother, who had added half an hour onto his time, would admonish him and he in his part would accept the scolding with grace. It was a game with the pecking order established and their bond reinforced.

"You can blame me this time if you want," he said.

"Is that so," smiled his father, "and what makes you think your mother would accept it. Thanks for the offer though."

Don't interrupt the game, thought Fred.

"Okay, it's your fault."

"That's more like it. I'm still the man of the house and I'll take it on the chin." He smiled and Fred found himself laughing. It had been too long. "More importantly, son, what are you going to do now?" His father was suddenly serious again and was looking at him.

"I hadn't really thought about it, all I really thought about was getting home or, if I'm being honest, away from all the madness. I did go a little mad myself you know, and I'm not proud of it." He felt odd admitting this but somehow relieved to confess it.

"That's understandable. You have to go a little mad to survive it. You're not the first but I hope to God you're the last. It's a pity that the people who cause the wars are never the ones who fight them. If they had to, they may be more reluctant to call them. Still, you've now got to get on with your life. Take my word, you'll never forget but you've got to put it behind you. Look to the future not the past. How about taking up your place at Teacher Training College. If nothing else, you could teach the next generation not to be so bloody stupid, even if you've got to beat it into them."

Fred realised that his father was talking about himself as much as him, and reliving his own experiences and it all became very clear to him who his father was. His determination to build a secure future for himself and his family, to protect them and be beholding to no man. To have respect and walk his own way.

"It's a thought," he said. It was, and at least it would give him a focus and a future. "I'll write to the college and see what they say."

"Good, don't leave it too long. Now, let's go before I get into any more trouble." With that, he got up and put on his coat. They left the pub, giving their thanks to the landlord as they went, and walked home side by side. For the first time in years, Fred felt secure but he now knew that even with a future he would never be free of the past or the nightmare he had lived. But for now, that would have to be enough.

As they reached the house, he entered first. "Sorry we're late, Mum, it's my fault."

"I very much doubt that," she replied smiling. His father was also smiling.

Chapter Sixteen

Fred did, in fact, write to the college, who were more than happy to enrol him, and at the end of the summer, he found himself in the old and historic city. It was in the days when the college still had dormitories but, for anyone used to barrack life, it was no hardship and for Fred, it was relative luxury after the jungle. But what he found difficult was mixing with his fellow students. He was used to dealing with hardened men and the youth entering education were too callow for his taste and beyond his understanding.

It didn't occur to him that they were mirrors of his younger self but he was becoming intolerant, a trait that would stay with him over the coming years. But he wasn't unkind and the others were more in awe of him than afraid, and in return he would look after them, keeping the dorm in line like the good sergeant he had been. But he missed having someone to confide in, someone who had had the same experiences, and in the end, sought solitude. This was also important as he had endured months of the smothering affection of his mother prior to leaving at the start of term. And so, at the latter end of the summer he took to roaming the streets of the city.

The city was a strange mix of historic, industrial and academic heritage. Small, it had city status due to its gothic cathedral and the presence of its looming castle. A medieval market town it had found itself at the centre of burgeoning heavy industry but had managed to retain its character as all around changed. The university had emerged during this time and brought in an influx of students from across the country, lending a cosmopolitan atmosphere to the city and adding a unique charm to the place. Fred enjoyed the narrow-cobbled streets that somehow muffled sound as it slowed the progression of both pedestrian and vehicle alike. It was still a working city but the centre belonged to the cathedral, the university and the old county bureaucracy with the workers terraces and cottages confined to the riverside and the rising hills. But its' cluttered and seemingly random structure hid another charm for Fred; a multitude of small public houses squashed in the terraces of the small streets, which he explored at his leisure and pleasure.

Fred had emerged from the jungle with two years back pay and that, together with various grants and low living costs meant he had plenty of money. He would say in his later years that he had spent every penny of it on beer. And that was true. Back home, and not wishing to upset his mother, he had been fairly constrained, but now he had no one to worry about and was enjoying his love of beer. He would never be an alcoholic as he avoided spirits and only drank on an evening. But he found that beer lifted his mood and stopped him, temporarily, from dwelling on the past. The college turned a blind eye on his activities as his work didn't suffer, and in truth, he was a very good student. The porters, on the other hand, may not have approved, but, used to chasing young boys, knew better than to tackle a veteran jungle fighter and paratrooper. So, he came and went as he pleased.

Fred had sampled most of the local hostelries when he'd first arrived, but had settled on the Bay Horse for several reasons. Primarily because the landlord kept good beer but also because it was small and quiet, a drinkers pub. It also had the benefit of being close to the college; before a central road was driven through the city a small lane ran from the college gate and up a narrow alley practically to the pub door. Despite all that, and an advantage for Fred, it was not popular with students and he was left in peace.

Fred's peace was disturbed one night when, as he stood at the bar, a hand fell on his shoulder, and a voice said, "It's Fred, isn't it?" Fred had turned to look at the speaker and recognised one of the young lecturers from the college who he'd briefly met before at a class. "What are doing here?" the voice continued, "I thought this place wasn't popular with students." Fred put a name to the face; Duncan, who had a bit of a reputation as a rogue but was well liked amongst the fraternity.

"That's why I like it here," he replied, "and besides, the beers good."

Duncan laughed, "I don't blame you for that, and I'll take your advice on the beer. Three more points of that please," he said to the landlord as he pointed at Fred's glass. Turning his head to Fred, he added, "You'll join us for one, won't you?" Fred looked at saw he was standing with a tall, quiet and handsome man.

"Of course," he replied, feeling he had little choice. Besides, he found he liked Duncan and, rarely, felt like company. "Who's your friend?"

"Sorry, I should have introduced you. This is Alex, we went to university together. He's here finishing his doctorate and working as a junior lecturer. I've been showing him around."

"What about you, Fred, you don't look like the average student." Alex spoke, he had a soft voice matched with a serious expression. Fred could have resented the question but accepted it as genuine interest.

"I'm not," he replied. "I've been away in the army. What about you?"

"Alex was in the war too," Duncan answered for him. "Right from the beginning as he was at Dunkirk. I was in North Africa and Italy. What about you?"

"Burma for my sins, the forgotten army." Fred didn't normally talk about the war or his experiences but felt comfortable being with men who'd been through the same thing. In fact, he felt comfortable for the first time in a long time.

"So, what made you come to the college?" It was Alex who spoke now, in his soft voice that only carried to the intended listeners ears. Fred respected that: he hated people whose conversations dominated a room which was why he didn't fraternise with students.

"It was what I intended doing before. When I came home, I wasn't sure where I was going or what I wanted. Everything was the same, but it wasn't if you know what I mean. I

91

suppose I'm trying to pick up the pieces, but you can never go back you know."

Alex laughed, not in a cruel way but one that was self-depreciating. "You're not alone there. We are exactly the same. All over this country, men are beginning to wonder what the hell it was all about and how do we get back to normality or, if we can. Duncan and I are the same, that's probably why we are here?"

"Speak for yourself, old boy," Duncan laughed, "I'm out for fun and if it isn't fun, I don't want it. And what I do want, in the absence of a good woman, is a good drink so get them in. Actually, I should have said a bad woman if you know what I mean."

"With me, it's a good woman, you old reprobate. But I'll get them in," said Alex.

"No, you won't," Fred jumped in. "It's my turn."

The three of them talked and drank for the rest of the evening, Duncan being jovial and the centre of attention whilst Alex sat quietly but occasionally asked a probing question. Fred liked this quiet man and didn't mind the conversation which covered his background and war experiences. He was actually relieved by his interest and the fact that someone actually cared about what had happened and what it had done to people. Alex was to become his conscious whilst Duncan would be the party host. This was to become a regular feature of Fred's time at college and would continue for years to come.

Chapter Seventeen

Alex had, indeed, been at Dunkirk. But he never spoke of it, or the rest of his war service. There was good reasons for this and his quiet approach to life. He'd joined up immediately at the outbreak of war and was commissioned as second lieutenant on the general list before being sent with the British Expeditionary Force to France. Initially, he was glad to be there, to be doing his bit in a place he loved. His mother was a Channel Islander and he had French relatives through her and many happy memories of holidays spent with them. In fact, he had spent so much time there that his French was practically fluent, and if his accent wasn't native, his vocabulary; through his love of books, was extensive.

He was still the gregarious and athletic man he had always been and was popular with both his men and the other officers. So, his early experiences; while the phony war continued, if not blissful, were at least relatively enjoyable. He sat out in the summer sun with his fellow officers, sharing wine and conversation. One among them, a young captain, was particularly impressed with his French. He was Anglo French and they often conversed in the language for both practice and enjoyment.

But the balmy days were to come to an end when, on the 10th May the Germans invaded the Netherlands and advanced westward. Plan D was initiated by the allies and they entered Belgium to engage the Germans in the Netherlands. The plan relied on the Maginot Line but the Germans had already crossed north of the Netherlands before the troops arrived. The troops were committed to the River Dyle but the enemy burst through the Ardennes before turning towards the

Channel in what became known as the 'Sickle Cut' effectively flanking the Allied forces.

A series of counter attacks followed, but failed to halt the German progress and they reached the coast on 20th May effectively separating the allied forces. Alex first saw action during these counter attacks and was shocked by the intensity of the fighting, the carnage all around and the horrific loss of life.

The advance stopped short of Dunkirk when the enemy decided to consolidate and avoid an allied breakout. A defensive line was thrown up around Dunkirk and the fighting began in earnest. At Wytschaete a holding action was made and a confused battle was fought in poor visibility and they were infiltrated and driven back. The route back to Dunkirk passed through the town of Poperinge where there was a bottleneck at a bridge over the Yser Canal where most of the roads converged.

Stuck in traffic, Alex witnessed the Luftwaffe bombing the convoy for two straight hours immobilising eighty percent of the vehicles. Further raids followed and many guns and Lorries had to be abandoned and the battle became a rout with them running for the coast harassed by the enemy.

But if Alex thought he had seen everything; the worst was still to come. They reached Dunkirk to find the town in chaos. Literally thousands of troops sat on the beach without direction as marshals tried to restore order. In between all this, planes were strafing the troops and canon shells were falling indiscriminately amongst them. Every day, more troops arrived to replace the fallen and the process continued.

Churchill would later proclaim the victory of Dunkirk as the armada of small ships arrived to evacuate the trapped with over three hundred thousand being rescued, but he didn't mention the bodies floating in the sea or those lying in pieces across the sand. Alex couldn't have put it better than the overheard response of a sergeant being helped out of a ship in Plymouth by a young recruit.

To his question 'how was it', his reply summed it up, "It was a complete cock up, son." Alex couldn't have put it better; it was a complete cock up. And a bloody one at that.

Chapter Eighteen

Alex was in London waiting, it seemed aimlessly, for a new posting. He'd headed for the city for want of something better to do, and it seemed the logical place to be as it was the heart of the military world. The streets seemed to team with uniformed bodies but he didn't feel a part of it; there was bizarrely an air of optimism about which to him seemed at odds with the facts of the situation and people were already talking about the Dunkirk spirit as if it had been a great victory rather than the debacle he'd experienced with all its accompanying slaughter.

He, therefore, spent his time wandering the streets which seemed grey and dismal with the lights blacked out. In search of some beauty, he'd headed down to the embankment, called at St Pauls and walked up to Holborn. Ready for a break, he'd gone into a local pub, ordered a beer and sat himself down at a table near the bar. He was lost in thought, half looking at the glass in front of him, when a coat was tossed onto the seat next to him and a voice said, "Bonjour, Mon Ami." There, in front of him, was his friend the young captain; now wearing majors crowns, from France.

"What brings you here, my friend?"

"Reorganisation. Waiting for a posting. And you, you appear to be doing all right. And a major to boot."

"Don't be fooled by that. I'm attached to headquarters, sort of, and badges are like confetti at a wedding. But why the glum face, you look as miserable as sin. Where's the jovial chap I knew so well?"

"I left him at Dunkirk with the rest of my illusions."

"So cynical for one so young. You need something to occupy you rather than sitting moping. What are you going to do?"

"Whatever I'm told to I suppose. I just hope it's better managed than the last fiasco."

His friend looked at him gravely, "You think Dunkirk was a fiasco?"

"Don't you. Every prediction we made was wrong and the Germans walked around us. We should have slowed them up but we were always in the wrong place. And when we moved, the logistics were so bad we got snarled up and were sitting ducks. Finally, the air cover was abysmal and we got bombed at will. If that's not a fiasco, I don't know what is."

"You think we should have had better intelligence."

"Of course. I was taught at university that conclusions should be based on facts and sound information, and that all consequences should be weighed before a decision was made."

"If that's how you feel would you be prepared to help getting that information?"

"Do you mean would I find it preferable to stumbling from disaster to disaster and leading men into other such messes? Then the answer would be yes. Wouldn't you?"

"Probably. But his is getting too serious for old friends. Let's have another drink. What do you want?"

"To hell with it. I'll have a whisky if they have it."

"Sound man." His friend bought two whiskies and they sat comfortably making small talk during which Michael, his friend, asked him about his background and his time at college. Alex realised he hadn't said anything about himself.

"What about you, you haven't said anything about yourself. You said you were attached to headquarters, sort of, what are you up to?"

"Next time, old boy. Look, if you're really interested in changing things, call at this address tomorrow at nine."

With that he grabbed his coat and was gone before Alex could ask what he meant. He stared at the piece of paper in front of him, non-descript and with a typed address on it. He knew the area it was in but didn't recognise it as any of the military offices he was familiar with. Intrigued, he put it in his pocket, put on his coat and headed home.

Chapter Nineteen

Alex turned up at the address Michael had given him; in Baker Street, a little before nine the following morning and was surprised to find it was the headquarters of a well-known retail chain. Curious he entered to find himself in an entrance lobby, all oak panels and dark carpets, with a reception desk at the end of the room. He approached it where a young woman was sifting papers.

Feeling awkward, he asked, "Excuse me, I'm wondering if I'm in the right building. I was asked to call here at nine."

"And your name, sir?"

"Lieutenant McIntyre."

For the first time, she smiled. "It's all right, you are in the right place and you are expected. If you take the lift over there to the third floor, turn right and walk down the corridor you'll come to another reception desk. Let them know you have an appointment with Mr Potter."

He did as he was told and went up in the antiquated lift to the third floor. Turning right he found himself in an improbably long and dark corridor lined with the same oak panelling. Walking down, he again wondered if he was in the right place when he saw a girl, dressed reassuringly in an ATS uniform, sitting at a desk outside a dark oak door.

When he went over, she looked up and said, "Good morning, Lieutenant McIntyre, Mr Potter is expecting you. If you give me a moment, I'll let him know you're here." She picked up a telephone, pressed a button and announced, "He's here, sir." Turning back to Alex, she said, "Please go in, lieutenant."

Alex went to the door indicated, another of the seemingly endless oak ones, and went in. He was surprised to see not a uniformed officer sitting behind the large wooden desk but a middle-aged man in a business suit, his slightly balding hair swept back with brilliantine. He seemed at ease in the room which was kept dark by the heavily patterned carpet on the floor. He indicated a seat on the opposite side of the desk.

"Please sit down and make yourself comfortable. Help yourself to a cigarette," he said as he pointed to a box on the desk. Alex did as he was requested and took a cigarette. Lighting it with a gold lighter from his pocket, he sat down. "Nice lighter," remarked his host.

"Present from my father," he replied.

"You'll have to watch for such things in future."

"Why is that, Mr Potter?" he asked somewhat confused. "I presume it is, Mr Potter?"

"For the time being, yes. But more of that later. I understand you were at Dunkirk. What did you think of it?" It was a question he wasn't expecting but he decided that he should be honest.

"It was a disaster. Badly planned, terrible intelligence and what should have been an orderly withdrawal turned into a compete rout. The Germans were left to their own devices and bombed us at will as we clogged up the roads."

"Strong views but I tend to agree. Rout is a very good description; the slaughter of troops as they try to escape the battlefield. You were a historian at college. A medievalist, I believe?"

"You're very well informed." Alex could feel his anger rising.

"Yes, we are. Please stay calm. Tell me what you think should be done differently in the future. I am interested in your opinion." Alex could feel himself being drawn in but his temper made him forthright and, besides, he had nothing to hide.

"Well, for a start, we need better intelligence, what is where, what strength is out there, what can be done to disrupt the enemy and how can we slow them down. A tall order, but if we want to win, we don't have a choice. The days of playing cricket are over. Not very gentlemanly, but then warfare isn't."

"I couldn't agree more. And what about you. Would you be prepared to do what is necessary?"

"If it could shorten this war, with victory, bring the Germans to heel, and end the slaughter the answer would be yes." Potter looked at him gravely and nodded.

"I can see you mean that. Would you be kind enough to wait outside please?" Alex realised the interview, if that was what it was, was over and he was being very politely asked to leave. He rose from his seat and crossed to the door. As he glanced back, he saw Potter reach for the telephone. Without a goodbye, he went back to the desk outside and spoke to the girl sitting there.

"I've been asked to wait." She gestured to a seat and he sat down wondering what had just occurred. Who was Mr Potter for the time being? Why was a civilian interviewing him and why did he have a uniformed secretary? And why was he in the headquarters of a department store. If he saw Michael again, he would have some explaining to do. As he thought this, as if on cue, Michael came striding up the corridor. Before he could say anything, Michael spoke.

"Well done, Captain McIntyre, please follow me." Before he could reply, Michael strode off and he was obliged to follow him. He went into another panelled door and Alex found himself in a similar office to the one he was in before.

"By the way, it's Lieutenant McIntyre." He thought he'd put the record straight right away.

Michael smiled, "I told you pips were like confetti around here. Welcome to the Baker Street Irregulars."

"I thought they were the street urchins used by Sherlock Holmes stories," asked a confused Alex.

Michael replied laughing, "That's the joke. We're only semi-official and don't really exist. We've been created to conduct espionage, sabotage and reconnaissance as part of the war effort. Our real name is the Special Operations Executive although some die-hards are already referring to us as the Ministry of Ungentlemanly Warfare. By the way, you almost gave Potter a heart attack when you said war wasn't gentlemanly."

"Well, it isn't, is it?"

"Quite, like I said, welcome to the irregulars."

Chapter Twenty

With new pips on his shoulders, Alex moved into Baker Street where he found himself working under Michael in the appropriately named F Section, the unit responsible for covert activity in France. Michael explained he had recommended Alex's recruitment based on his experiences at Dunkirk, his knowledge of France, fluency in the language, academic training and lastly, and most importantly, his conviction that a different approach was needed to win the war.

Alex found the executive a paradox; on the one hand it seemed to have the power; afforded by Churchill's enthusiasm for the organisation, to move things very quickly. On the other, it appeared to be in total chaos, having goals but little in the way of delivering them. He soon found out that this was one of the reasons he had been recruited. The selection of agents remained the responsibility of the redoubtable Mr Potter, but their initial training, assessment, specialist training and assignment fell to the rest of the section which basically fell under Michael's shoulders. If a daunting task, it was, at least an exciting one which the team, including Alex, greeted with enthusiasm.

It was early days for the section and essential that the right agents were recruited. Although Mr Potter made the selection, their suitability was under further, and constant, scrutiny. To this end, Alex found himself more and more at the old manor house in Surrey the section had acquired that became STS5 where new recruits were sent to whittle out those not suited for undercover work and to begin initial training for those who progressed.

This was for a three- or four-week period during which they were trained in the skills required for such work including unarmed combat and the art of silent killing, Successful trainees were also kitted out with the necessary clothes and identity documents and received the latest information on what was happening in France and, if required, their French was improved. Those who successfully passed the four-week course at the manor were sent to Scotland for further instruction on using small arms and explosives. Lastly, they received parachute training.

Alex found it was his job to oversee the process, delivered by specialists, and ensure that agents were both ready and suitable for the missions required of them. In the early days, it was a bit like the phoney war, all enthusiasm and expectation but when missions began and agents started to fail to return, reality started to bite. This affected them all and led them to an even greater aloofness with agents. Trainers passed recruits on very quickly but handlers who developed a rapport with them had a more difficult task. Alex, who saw them from application to mission maintained a distance, not cold, but professional, in spite of his fascination with their characters. And fascinating they were too; especially the women, from the athletic no nonsense Australian who killed an enemy soldier with her bare hands whilst on a mission, to the quiet girl who turned out to be the best shot they ever trained. But he kept his distance until Helene arrived.

Helene was a stunning woman, dark, fine featured and petite. This was matched by an independent spirit and fiery determination. She was of Anglo-French parentage; her father having met her mother whilst he was serving in the First World War. Born in France, she had lived there during her formative years, only moving to London in her early teens. As such, she was not only fluent in French but spoke with an authentic accent and it was that which had first brought her to the attention of SOE.

At that time, like many patriotic French women, she had joined the ATS to assist in the fight to liberate Europe. On recruitment, she was commissioned as a Section Leader in the First Aid Nursing Yeomanry: the affectionately named FANYS, a civilian service often used by SOE as a cover for female agents. It was also a way to towards complying with the Geneva Convention that women in the services should not bear arms. After initial induction, she received intensive training in the use of weapons, escape and evasion, unarmed combat, night and daylight navigation, demolition explosives, communications and cryptography.

Alex oversaw her training and her readiness for active service. He maintained a professional distance from her, as he did with other operatives, but at the same time, took more than a passing interest in her development and deployment. Helene for her part was a little confused by his interest; men had always been attracted to her and she was used to their attention and, to be frank, enjoyed it. But, unlike them, he never pursued matters further which fascinated her. He was after all, an attractive man and cultured. But his distance made him even more fascinating and he began to fill her thoughts.

Chapter Twenty-One

All thoughts of Alex were pushed to one side as she was parachuted into France near Cherbourg with the task of reorganising a network of French resistance that had been smashed by the Germans. She led the group in sabotaging road and rail bridges and sent wireless reports to SOE headquarters on the local factories which were producing war materials for the Germans. Her arrival set the tone of the relations she was to have with the Frenchmen she worked with when her parachute snagged on a tree in an orchard.

The man sent to meet her glanced up and remarked, "Ah the trees are yielding beautiful fruits this season."

To which he received the reply, "And you can cut that French shit and get me down." He did as requested and did as he was told after that.

Helene worked hard at establishing the network and gained the respect of her Maquis colleagues for her bravery in the field and tenacity in gleaning information to send back to headquarters. This was vital in establishing Allied bombing targets and her reports; under her codename Ivy, were eagerly anticipated. This was none more so than by Alex whose initial interest in the success of her mission turned gradually into concerns for her ongoing safety. Her stay became protracted and his anxiety grew. But the success was too great to curtail the mission.

Things came to a head when the car she was travelling in was stopped by the French police and she was arrested. When questioned, she managed to convince them she posed no danger and was released. However, she realised the game was nearly up and made her way to Paris where she requested a pick up. She returned to England on a Westland Lysander and was met at the airfield by Alex who was to debrief her. As she descended from the plane, her emotions were confused. She was relieved to be home and safe but that relief was tainted by the release of the tensions and stress she had accumulated on the mission and she felt drained and weary. No longer having to act and be always alert, she stumbled and was caught by Alex.

As she straightened and looked up to thank him, she became more confused. Expecting a rebuke, she saw a look of genuine concern on his face turning to a hint of joy at seeing her which was quickly hidden as his professional mask was put back on. For Helene, her joy at seeing him again suffused her with energy.

Straightening herself up, she said, "It's good to see you again."

"You too," he replied.

Together, they walked side by side to the office, which was little more than a wooden shed, at the edge of the runway where he listened to her account of her experiences and noted the information he would pass on to the appropriate agencies. The debrief took a while as he listened to her story which would help other agents in the field, but it was more that he was enjoying her company that held his attention. After a while, he noticed her shiver; it was a cold night and the hut was drafty.

"Come with me," he said, "it's too late to go to London and there's nowhere on the airfield to stay. I've booked you a room at a small pub we use. Besides, I think we both could use a drink." She nodded.

Chapter Twenty-Two

The pub was a delightful old stone built and white washed structure with sash windows set below eaves. Roses grew up the walls adding a pleasant aroma and warm ambiance to the building. It was late when they arrived and the place was empty but a soft glow came from the lower window. They were expected as they had a regular arrangement with the landlord who asked no questions but was happy to help in his own way in the war effort as he was too old to fight. He met them at the door; a balding middle-aged man with a landlords flushed face and a paunch held in by his waistcoat, a slightly shabby man but still with a respectful collar and tie.

"Come in," he welcomed them, "I took the liberty of keeping some supper for you. Can I get you a drink while you're waiting?"

"That would be splendid," Alex replied. "And we'll just eat here in the lounge. I'll have a whisky if I may. Helene, what would you like?" She was taken aback the casual use of her name and somewhat pleased.

"I'll have the same if you'll be so kind."

Bert smiled, "For you people, nothing is too much trouble. Please take a seat and I'll bring them over."

A short while later, they found themselves sitting at a small table in an alcove sipping their whiskies, enjoying the pleasant warm feeling suffusing them as the tension was slowly released.

"How are you feeling now," he asked.

"Tired," she replied, "and a little strange. It's a little odd sitting here as if there isn't a war going on and not looking over your shoulder all the time to see whose watching and listening to you so that you're always conscious of what you are saying. This is a bit surreal to be honest, pleasant but surreal." She looked at him as she said this with a small smile on her lips. Before he could reply, the landlord appeared carrying a tray with two plates of food.

"It's game pie my wife made earlier. In the country, one thing we aren't short of is rabbits," he laughed, "is that all right?"

"I'm sure it will be perfect." And it was, beautiful short crust pastry covering game in a rich gravy and accompanied by fresh vegetables. Helene pushed her empty plate aside with a sigh. "That's the best I've eaten in months," she said with a satisfied smile on her lips.

"Good, Bert makes sure we're looked after. He's a good sort. Was it rough over there? I was worried about you." She was surprised, but pleased by his admission.

"Were you?" She saw him blush slightly and fluster.

"Of course, I always worry when we send an agent out. I'm happy to have you back."

"Are you really. You don't have to worry about me now." She smiled and laid her hand on his as she said this. She noticed with satisfaction that he was in no hurry to move it away.

Still holding her hand, he said, "If you don't mind, I think I'll worry about you a little longer." He was also smiling, no longer blushing and looking directly into her eyes. They sat like this for a long time, hands touching and eyes locked sipping their drinks which Bert had quietly replaced unbidden.

They were still like this when Bert returned and coughed discretely, "Your rooms are ready. You must be tired?"

"Are you?" Alex asked her.

"A little, it's been a long day." They followed Bert up the narrow stairs to two doors at the end of a short landing.

He stopped, "This is yours, sir, the lady is next door. I hope that's suitable?"

"Perfectly fine," Helene replied and went into her room and Alex, after a moment's pause went into his. The room was simple but pleasant with moonlight entering through the open curtains. Alex closed them and was just reaching for the lamp switch when the door opened and Helene walked into the room. "I forgot to say goodnight." Looking directly at him, she added, "Now what are you going to do about this?" Alex said nothing as he walked across the room and took her in his arms and kissed her.

In the early morning, Alex lay with Helene's head resting on his chest. The dawn light was coming though the partially opened curtains and he gazed at her pretty face framed by curling hair. He'd had girlfriends before but he'd never had his desires met with such passion. He lay there for a long time just drinking her in until propriety returned. With gentle nudging, she awakened and looked up sleepily at him.

Her hand stroked his chest, "That's the best sleep I've had in a long time. Can we not just stay like this?"

There was nothing he wanted more but life was complicated. "We need to get up and head back to town." He grinned, "And what will Bert think?"

"You silly man, Bert is not that stupid. But to spare your feelings, I'll go back to my room to get ready." As she reached the door, she turned back and grinned, "I'll even ruffle my bed to spare your blushes. Don't forget, I'm good at this subterfuge. See you downstairs."

A short while later, they, after saying goodbye to Bert, sat side by side in the front seats of the car as they headed back to London. It was a warm spring day with a blue sky and dappled sunlight. With the exception of an overenthusiastic home guard patrol who stopped them at a checkpoint, the journey was uneventful. Even that was only a minor inconvenience, his captain's uniform and papers granted them immediate respect and they were en route within minutes. In many ways, it was, as Helene said, like a drive out for a summers picnic. It was also the way a love affair should begin, and it happened that way.

Back in London Alex dropped her at the small Notting Hill flat she was renting with a promise to come back later. It was a promise he kept repeatedly and the small flat became their love nest. All the while, they were careful to keep their relationship a secret knowing it would be frowned upon by higher command. Alex was certain that Michael suspected their romance but had decided to keep quiet about it. In return, Alex didn't flaunt it. When they went out together; which was rare as they generally were happy to stay in, it was never in London.

When possible, they would drive out to coaching houses in the Home Counties, out of the way and out of the way of prying eyes, just a captain on leave enjoying time with his wife. There they could be themselves and eat and dance together. Alex, to her delight, was a good dancer as they whirled together. They even discovered their own song. As they danced one evening, the refrain came with the music, "There are bluebirds in the moonlight, silly idea bluebirds in the moonlight, but that's how I feel when I'm with you."

Helen looked at him, "That sums us up, this is a silly idea, but not when I'm with you." A blissful spring turned into a beautiful summer and that's when Alex had the idea that they should stop pretending and get married.

It wasn't as pragmatic as that, he did actually get onto to one knee with a ring in hand. Helene answered as he expected, that she would love to but they would have to wait until the war was over and their duties permitted. He was ready for this, "The war will be over soon, and our duties are coming to an end I wouldn't ask otherwise, but I want you to be my wife now." At this, she smiled and said yes.

Subterfuge training came in useful as they planned their marriage, which took place at a small registry office in a little market town away from London. Two of Helene's old friends; with no office connections, acted as witnesses and no other guests were present. But they didn't need any, they were together, two souls caught in a gathering storm.

Chapter Twenty-Three

But Alex's assertion that their involvement in the war was coming to an end proved to be short lived as he was summoned to Michael's office as the first troops were landing on the beach in Normandy.

"Take a seat, Alex," he said to a surprised Alex. He and Michael had never used much formality beyond a basic respect for rank in the decision-making process. "We've had a request to send an agent to France."

"At this stage, why? The troops have landed and are moving forward."

"That's the whole point. We need someone to coordinate the activities of the local Maquis to sabotage the German communication lines and help the advance." Alex was apprehensive as Michael continued, "And we need to send Helene."

Michael's use of Helene's real name triggered alarms in Alex's mind. "You mean Ivy?"

"Come off it," said Michael looking straight at him. "I've known for some time you and Helene were getting close. But I chose to ignore it because I thought her operational days were at an end. But she's not only the most qualified for the mission but the only person I have available."

Alex knew he was beaten, it was what she was trained for, what she had volunteered for and what she wanted to do. So, he merely nodded.

"Look at the bright side, this will be all over quickly, she'll be back before you know it and then you can make this official and stop hiding."

Official, thought Alex, *you don't even know the half of it.*

Helene took the news of her mission stoically in her usual calm manner whilst Alex looked on. Later on, she tried to reassure him, as Michael had, "Don't worry, I'll be back before you know it."

"Don't make light of it," he replied angrily. "You know the dangers and I don't want to lose you."

"You won't, and I'll come back to you. You'll see. You know I have no choice and neither do you. We'll be okay."

"I know but that doesn't make it any easier. Just take care."

She promised she would and again when she boarded the plane that was to parachute her ahead of the troops. She was dropped near Limoges where she worked with the local resistance disrupting enemy communications ahead of advances. As fate would have it, she was in a car that raised the suspicions of German troops at an unexpected roadblock. A gun battle ensued where she fought valiantly until her Sten gun ran out of ammunition. Her cover allowed her Maquis colleagues to escape but she was captured and taken to Gestapo headquarters where she was intensively interrogated, tortured, sexually assaulted, raped and beaten severely. But she refused to give away any information. She was then transferred to a concentration camp where she was executed at the beginning of 1945.

When news of her capture reached F Section, Alex was distraught, blaming himself for letting her go and taking every opportunity to scour reports to find her. When news of her death reached them, his world finally collapsed. Michael had watched his decline with increasing concern. He'd commiserated with him when the news first arrived, but, for all his knowledge of their closeness, it was more in the nature of when a colleague was lost.

Finally, he said to him, "Look, Alex, I'm sorry we lost her but we have to move on. If it's too much for you, would you like me to contact her next of kin?"

"You're looking at him," he replied. "We were married, your intelligence wasn't that good." Michael didn't know what to say, what could he. Alex left the army as soon as he could after that, never looking back. He never attended reunions; it was far too painful. Nor would he ever forget her, in his heart, she would always be his wife.

Chapter Twenty-Four

Alex's life was very much in the present as he stood with Duncan and Fred in a pub in the old part of the city. The pub was deceptively small from the front but a warren of small rooms to the rear. Its front bar was narrow and therefore, always seemingly full. This didn't bother the men as they were used to standing, and besides, they didn't intend on staying for the full evening having other plans. Since they had all met Fred had qualified as a teacher and was now working at one of the village schools on the outskirts of the city. The school could be described as rough but as an ex-paratrooper and *chindit,* he didn't intimidate easily and commanded respect from both his students and their parents and, indeed, a certain amount of grudging affection.

Alex, on the other hand, had devoted himself to his studies and was now Doctor McIntyre, a title he could now add to the rank of major he had left the army with. Not that he ever used, or even referred to it. He was now regarded as a serious academic and lived very quietly. His father had recently died and he had moved into his house on the edge of the city, which was oddly just a few miles from the village where Fred was teaching.

Duncan was still at the university and the old pub, on the approach to the castle and Cathedral, was where gown met town. It was not their regular haunt; although paradoxically it was reputedly the most haunted pub in the city. But today, it was on the way to an old hall on the approach to the Cathedral which, following its requisition during the war, now provided a venue for dances.

Fred was stood happily by the bar, becoming more jovial as he drank from the pint glass in his hand. During the week, he still went out but was conscious of school the next day and restricted what he drank. But on a weekend, those rules no longer applied and he was prone to excess.

"What time are we going?" he said to Duncan.

"About 15 minutes," Duncan replied.

"Good, time for a quick one, three more pints please, Bella," he shouted across the bar.

"Not for me," Alex interrupted the order, "I've had enough. Besides, we don't want to keep the ladies waiting." He turned to Duncan. "Will Ruby be okay until we get there?"

"Yes, she's with her friend. Nice girl, they worked together in Italy. When they were demobbed, they both joined the civil service and she followed Ruby up here. Their renting a small house together in the city."

"Must be cramping your style?" smiled Alex.

"Not necessarily," Duncan grinned back. "But you're right, I'd better not upset her. We'll go as soon as I've finished my drink."

With that he gulped his beer down and, dragging a protesting Fred, they fell out of the door into the dark street. The dim street lamps illuminated the pub sign and its' leaded windows lit from inside. It was a still, damp night with a mist glistening off the cobbled street as, tumbling merrily against each other, they walked up the steep street towards the Cathedral green. A terrace of old Georgian town houses lined the street as shops, with the exception of the university bookshop, had not yet reached this part of the city; most of which belonged to either the university or the church and were tied for academics and clergy. Duncan still lived here but Alex had given up his accommodation when he'd moved to his father's house although he still kept rooms in his college to meet with students.

They walked uphill until they reached, just before the Cathedral green, a large house, built originally to house the castle guards. Once a domestic residence, it had been requisitioned during the war and used by the Women's Reserve Club to serve lunches to the public. It was now used by various groups and was also the venue for local dances which was why it was their destination for the evening. Like many of the buildings in the street, it still incorporated part of the old castle walls and was deceptively large inside; its length defying its outside width. As they entered the outer door, they found themselves at the beginning of a long corridor running straight through the length of the building. Music filtered down from the end, but before then a side door opened onto a kitchen and small tearoom where Ruby sat at a table with her friend Ivy.

Duncan went straight over to them and, leaning over, kissed her on the cheek. "Have you been here long?"

"Not really," she replied. "I knew you'd have to go for a drink first so we allowed extra time. And don't deny it, I can smell it on your breath."

"Just a quick one," he said sheepishly. "You wouldn't deny the boys that?"

"Or two or three perhaps?" Alex smiled at the exchange. Duncan's relationship with Ruby was something of a mystery. With other women, he was charming, and if truth were known, somewhat predatory. It wasn't something he secretly approved off but tolerated out of friendship. But with Ruby, he was caring and obedient; at least when he was with her. Alex could still, at times, see the quiet boy he had originally known and suspected that he was still in there somewhere but that only Ruby could touch him. However, Alex was a fatalist and what would be would be, and in the meantime, Duncan was good company and Alex needed that.

Ruby was a different matter. If anything, she was stern and somewhat intimidating. Not that Alex could be intimidated or bullied, but she was difficult to warm to. But for all her shrewishness and shortness with him, it was clear she doted on Duncan like a mother with a much loved, but errant son, at times scolding but always forgiving.

The thought struck Alex suddenly, that was exactly what it was like, she the mother and Duncan the naughty but adored child. Shocked by this revelation, he turned his attention to Ivy who he'd never met before and saw a petite pretty girl with light brown hair and smiling eyes. He wondered what she could have in common with Ruby but was later to discover that Ruby didn't make friends as such but rather adopted people, controlling but maternal.

As no introductions were forthcoming, he thought he'd better make the effort himself. "Hello," he said holding out his hand, "I'm Alex, an old friend of Duncan's."

She took his hand in hers which was pleasantly warm. "Pleased to meet you, I've heard a lot about you, I'm Ivy." Alex felt his heart sink; Ivy, Helene's code name. She was never far from his thoughts but came rushing back at that moment.

To change the subject, he turned, and motioning to Fred, said, "And this reprobate is Fred." Ivy looked and saw a well-dressed, but slightly dishevelled figure standing next to Alex. He was smaller than Alex but muscular and had obviously drank more than his friends. He wasn't bad looking but she preferred the more elegant and refined Alex. Alex was also more attuned to others feelings and decided to move things on.

"Come on, you lot. I thought we came to dance." Laughing, they stood up and followed him down the narrow corridor to where the music was coming from. As they went, the music got louder until they came to a final door at the end and opening it went down several steps into a larger room at the end of the which of which a six-piece band was playing dance music. They found seats against a far wall and listened for several minutes until a young woman got up in front of the band and, as they struck up Honeysuckle Rose began to sing in the style of Mildred Bailey.

Alex, ever polite, held out his hand to Ivy, "Would you like to dance?" Ivy had been waiting for the invite and walked on to the floor. Alex, taking hold of her, moved smoothly to the music; he was of the generation where men were expected to be able to lead a woman across the dance floor and they moved well together. Ivy was happy; Ruby had brought her deliberately to meet Alex, a gentleman completely unlike Duncan.

The singer had sat down and they danced to several more tunes until the singer reappeared and began to sing Bluebirds in the Moonlight. As the lyrics 'there are bluebirds in the moonlight, silly idea bluebirds in the moonlight but that's how I feel when I'm with you' rang out, she felt Alex stiffen.

"Do you mind if we sit this one out?" he said as he led her from the floor. Confused, she nodded her head and they returned to their seats. Fred had been watching and had seen the look on her face as she sat down, confusion mixed with hurt.

"Come on, old girl, if this old man can't dance, I will," and held out his hand. Ivy would normally have refused, but was both hurt and cross at being rejected so took the proffered hand and followed him onto the floor. She found that Fred was surprisingly light on his feet if a little exuberant in his dancing. But it matched in with his character which was actually fun loving. She was to find out later that there was another side to him and that he used alcohol to hide from it but that would come later. In the meantime, he whirled her around and she found herself laughing at his antics.

"Are you at the university?" she asked.

"Nothing so grand, I'm afraid," he replied. "I studied there but now teach for my sins at a secondary school. Still it's a living."

"And an admirable one." She realised there was more to him than was at first apparent and began to enjoy herself.

Alex, who was watching them, touched Duncan on the arm and whispered that he needed to go. Duncan said nothing, merely nodded as Alex slipped through the door unseen. Alex was in pain, it wasn't that he didn't like Ivy, in fact he found her a lovely girl. He thought he could cope with the name but when bluebirds started playing, it was as if Helene was speaking to him. It had always been their song; they'd fallen in love to it when it was silly to do so and the lyric had amused them both. He'd felt guilty for betraying her memory and confused over his feelings. If he'd thought about it logically, he would have realised that Helene would have laughed at him and told him to get on with life but his heart said different. And so, he crept away which was to become his habit over the years. Ivy didn't notice his absence until she sat back down.

Chapter Twenty-Five

Ivy was confused; Ruby had taken her to the dance with the intention of introducing her to Alex. She had described him as a lovely man which in itself was a complement as Ruby liked very few people and men in general. Ivy knew she regarded Alex as a steadying influence on Duncan which in itself spoke volumes. Ivy had taken up the invitation not because she was desperate for a suitor but out of curiosity. As such, she had been pleasantly surprised when she'd met him; he was not only handsome but charming in a quiet way, so different from Duncan's brashness.

She'd enjoyed his company and was frankly hurt when he'd left without saying goodbye. And then Fred had waltzed her onto the dance floor when Alex had unexpectedly sat down. If she was honest with herself, she'd gone because she was annoyed with his behaviour and didn't wish to show that she cared. Fred had held no attraction for her when they'd been introduced, he was not her type and he'd obviously been drinking which on this occasion she disapproved of; he knew he'd be meeting them and it was, therefore, discourteous.

But when he'd taken to the floor, he'd been full of fun and a joy to be with. They'd danced most of the night and she was delighted to find him light on his feet and that her toes were safe. When the last slow dance of the evening had ended, she found, to her surprise, that she was a little disappointed. It was agreed that Duncan would see them home as Fred lived in the opposite direction and she was both surprised and delighted when Fred had asked her very quietly and gently if he could see her again. Carefully, she'd said yes and given him her address. With that, they had taken their leave and watched as Fred walked away.

Ruby, ever blunt, said on the walk back, "You and Fred seem to be getting on well?"

"He was surprisingly nice," she'd replied carefully. "Rather sweet actually."

"Be careful of that one, he's a bit too fond of a drink if you ask me."

"Fred's okay," Duncan interrupted. "He likes a drink like everyone else but he holds down a good job and his war record is pretty impressive." Ivy was intrigued and a little impressed how he leapt to his friend's defence against Ruby's scorn. He didn't usually contradict her.

"Well, you would defend him, wouldn't you," she responded tartly, but let the matter drop. They'd continued home silently after that, leaving Ivy time to think. She'd enjoyed herself, it was true, but reflected that it was unlikely she'd either see Alex again and that if she did, it was unlikely there would be any romantic attachment between them. As regards Fred, she decided he was fun to be with but that was as far as it went.

If Ivy thought that Fred was just fun, she discovered he had other ideas when she received a letter from him on the Monday morning. She knew he must have written it immediately after leaving her and posted it on the Saturday. She was both surprised and flattered by his attention and equally surprised by the polite tone of his letter. She reread it several times and drew the conclusion that here was a man who was unaccustomed to courting women; the very antithesis to Duncan who she saw as an arch seducer. She knew that her friendship with Ruby protected her from his advances but equally knew that without such a restraint, he wouldn't be able to resist a charm offensive.

He seemed to need the actual challenge, she thought, rather than the conquest itself. Fred, however, she concluded, was unsure of himself and that endeared him. She wrote back the same day and said she would be delighted to meet him again. A further letter arrived on the Wednesday asking her to meet him for tea on the Saturday to which she agreed. Ruby remarked that she seemed to be getting a lot of post to which she replied that it was merely an old school friend keeping in touch. She could tell Ruby didn't believe her but was reluctant to share any further details.

Fred, on the other hand, had no such reservations. When he met Duncan and Alex on that Friday for a drink, he was more reticent than usual. Duncan, as usual, was too concerned with himself to notice anything was wrong but Alex, ever sensitive to others moods, sensed that he had something on his mind.

"What's keeping you so quiet he asked? You're not even enjoying your beer as much."

"I've got a lot on my mind if you must know."

"Do you want to talk about it?" Alex could tell that Fred needed to share what was bothering him.

"Yes, to be honest. I've done something and I don't know what to do about it. I've written to Ivy and asked to see her again and she's said yes. I must admit, I'm really surprised. I thought, to be honest, that she had eyes for you and only stepped in when you buggered off and left her alone. You don't mind, do you?" Alex had to admit to himself that he had felt a momentary pang when Fred said this, if anything for an opportunity lost, but he still loved Helene and always would. But he also saw the absolute forlorn look on his friends face and felt immediate sympathy.

"Of course, I don't mind. She's a lovely girl and I don't blame you for wanting to see her." He saw the look of relief on Fred's face and couldn't resist a jibe. "As long as you don't take her to a pub."

"As if I would," laughed Fred. More seriously, he added, "where do you think I should take her?"

"When and what time are you meeting her?"

"Tomorrow afternoon. What do you think?"

"The times perfect. If the weathers good, take her for a walk by the river then find somewhere nice for afternoon tea. I mean somewhere nice, she's a refined girl and needs treating well."

"I agree, and I'll do just that." Decision made, Fred was back to his usual self and full of bounce. "What was that about beer? Let's have another, it's my round, what do you want?"

"Another pint would be nice. But watch what you're drinking, you don't want to be turning up tomorrow with a bad head and foul breath."

"I can handle it, you know that." Alex did know that but was amused when Fred started slowing down and finished the evening with a small whisky that he strung out, more content to hold it than drink it.

The boy's in love, mused Alex.

Chapter Twenty-Six

Fred met Ivy on the Saturday afternoon, bathed, groomed and somewhat apprehensive. More importantly, he was totally sober although he would have loved a drink to calm his nerves. But he didn't need a drink; even in his darkest hours, he had never retreated to it, he met his fears head on. No, when he drank, it was for another reason, it was to make him forget. Fred could face any physical challenge without fear, but it was the night time demons that he found difficult to handle and the nightmares they delivered. But however scared he might be today; he was determined to make a good impression. He was like a teenager on a first date and that wasn't too far from the truth: Ivy had been right when she'd thought he'd had little experience of courtship.

He'd grown up in the company of men in the barbarity of war and the dispensing of violence, not in the softness and kindly gestures of romance. Romance had been the last thing on his mind when he'd met Ivy, he was still smarting at having been pulled out of the pub, but Duncan and Fred were his friends and he still retained loyalty to that concept. But Ivy had awakened something in him; he'd drank enough to be carefree and had found her fun to be with and comforting to embrace. She'd filled the emptiness in him and he needed that. But now, in the cold light of day, he was less sure of himself and desperate not to be rejected.

He was lost in these thoughts as he'd leant on the statue in the middle of the market square; a familiar meeting place in the city, and only saw her approach at the last moment. She was dressed in a floral summer dress and white sandals and took his breath away, so he was barely able to respond to her greeting.

"Hello," she said, "have you been waiting long?"

"No, only a few moments," he lied. He'd been there over a quarter of an hour, anxious during the long wait but afraid he'd miss her.

"Good," she replied, "I didn't want to keep you waiting but didn't want to stand here on my own. Is that awful?"

"No, perfectly understandable. You can meet some strange types around here."

"As long as you're not one of them." She saw him grimace and instantly regretted her jest; he was, as she suspected, very insecure under that gruff exterior. To change the subject, she asked quickly, "What have you got planned for the day?"

Relieved, he said, "It's a beautiful day so I thought a walk by the river would be nice and maybe tea later."

"It sounds perfect." She meant it and he silently thanked Alex for his advice. She demurely hooked his left arm as they strolled across the market place and down the cobbled street lined with shops until they reached a narrow flight of stairs that led down to the river itself. At the bottom, they found themselves on the path that led though the grassy bank and past the old fulling mill. Further along, they passed the boathouses belonging to the rowing clubs who sculled on the river. Walking in amiable silence, they rounded the peninsular where the river changed direction until they reached a small building resplendent with classical columns.

"What's that?" she asked with genuine interest, "it's beautiful but somewhat out of place."

"It's the little count's house. Or to be more precise, his summerhouse. If you look up the bank, you can see a row of houses running along the top where he lived."

"Was he really a count?"

"Oh, yes, although the title wasn't English. He was actually a musician who performed for royalty and who settled here until he died."

"So why little?"

"Because he was a dwarf. If memory serves correctly, he's still holds the record as the longest living dwarf. Anyway, I like the title little count. It's a lot more attractive than the other local name for this stretch of the river."

"What's that?"

"It's known as the monkey walk. Why, I'm not quite sure but it's where demobbed soldiers from the last war used to walk with their girlfriends."

"Is that how you view me?" She'd decided she actually liked Fred, but refused to be taken for granted and was quite annoyed by any such assumption he might make.

"Of course not, I mean I just wanted to be with you, I think you're wonderful and," his words came out in a rush, practically incoherent as they were jumbled together, but all the more flattering for their sincerity. Ivy was taken aback by his genuine honesty and felt a little guilty for chastising him. She was too familiar fending off smooth men; especially the young officers she and Ruby had met during their service days. Honesty was not a trait she was used to but was somewhat refreshing. As they were approaching the main centre of the city, she saw in the distance the old boathouse with its collection of rowing boats for hire moored along the riverbank.

"Come on," she said to lighten the atmosphere, "you can take me out onto the river and show me how strong you are." Laughing, she skipped ahead forcing Fred to run after her. By the time he caught up with her, he was less abashed and, paying the fee, helped her gently into the boat before stepping in himself and pushing away from the bank. It seemed he'd taken her words literally and rowed manfully up the river. But what he displayed in vigour was offset by his lack of finesse in handling the boat. Ivy couldn't help but giggle at his antics.

At first, he seemed affronted, but joined in with laughter of his own, especially when she jokingly admonished his energetic rowing, "Be careful I've already had a bath today." The upset of earlier was forgotten as they spent a pleasant, and more tranquil, hour skimming the riverbank. The sun was out and the river was placid as they finally returned to the boathouse with flushed cheeks.

Stepping from the boat Ivy turned to Fred and asked him, "What's next?" She suspected he had been carefully planning the day and didn't want to disappoint him.

"It's a surprise," he said as he led her up the steep steps from the riverbank and back into the narrow and ancient cobbled streets of the city. As they walked up towards the cathedral, he pointed upwards. Following his gaze, she saw a copper teapot mounted high up on the wall by a narrow alleyway between the buildings. She was amazed she'd never seen it during her walks around the city.

"It's just up here," he said taking her arm. She let him lead her up the alley to where a door opened from the left wall. He gallantly held the door open and she entered a small teashop with whitewashed walls, dark wood tables and chairs; the chairs having embroidered cushioned seats and the tables resplendent with crisp white tablecloths. The room had an ancient but comfortable air about it and although sheltered was pleasantly light.

"This is lovely," she said with genuine feeling. "How did you find it?"

"I came across it during my student days." That was a lie, he'd asked all the staff at school and the consensus had been that this was the place to go. But he didn't want her to think he was too keen as he was still smarting inside over her previous rebuff. "It's a bit of a hidden gem."

"You're right about that. I would never have found it on my own. Thank you so much for bringing me. I must admit I was a little worried you might take me to a pub." His mind drifted back to Alex's previous comment and was shocked about his apparent reputation, he liked a drink but it wasn't his master.

"I only drink to forget," he said.

"What are you trying to forget?" she asked seriously.

"I don't know, I've forgotten."

She laughed, "That was almost a joke. I like it when you relax."

"Good. Anyway, I want to remember this day. I can relax with you and I like it." A waitress appeared and led them to a small table and took their order for high tea for two.

She smiled at him over the table, "I'm pleased you can relax with me. Why do you have trouble relaxing the rest of the time? I understand you had a difficult war. Is that it?"

126

"My war was no worse than a lot of men's." She could see he wasn't telling the truth but trying to present the proverbial stiff upper lip, men weren't supposed to have feelings and be weak. But she had seen too many boys in Italy who had been broken to believe that.

"You were in Burma, weren't you? I've read the reports. It was bloody in the truest sense of the word."

"You've no idea." Fred was suddenly quiet and very serious. Her heart went out to him.

"So why don't you tell me." She reached over and took his hand as she said this. He looked surprised, but didn't pull away so she squeezed his hand further.

"Okay," he said. "I expected action but it was brutal, pure slaughter at the end. I saw my best friend butchered next to me. I'll never forget the look on his face as he died. It still haunts me in the night. After that I went a little mad, kept telling myself to make them pay. I wasn't a very nice person then but I just kept telling myself I was just doing my duty. And then Imphal happened. The Japanese just kept attacking even as we mowed them down. It was what the Americans call a turkey shoot and the more we killed the more came. In the end, the ground was covered with their bodies. There was no one to take them away and we couldn't move so we watched them become bloated in the heat. I didn't know bodies could explode." She saw him shudder at the recollection. "It did me one favour, I lost the desire to kill and also hate. I remember my father being reluctant to talk about the last war and how he looked with pity at the broken men. I'm sorry, I shouldn't have told you all this."

"Of course, you can tell me." With insight, she saw the enthusiastic boy who had leapt to volunteer and how horror had, and still did, tortured him. Her heart went out to that young man.

"I've never told anyone this before. I'm sorry, I shouldn't burden you. It's not very manly."

"That's rubbish. It doesn't help keeping this in. You need to talk about his and you can always talk to me."

"I'm only telling you because I feel safe with you."

"You're always safe with me." Just then the waitress arrived with their tea. "Enough for now, we're having a lovely day out and thank you for that. Come on, let's enjoy the day."

"You're right," he smiled, "I'll even be mother." He reached for the pot and poured the tea to her laughter.

Chapter Twenty-Seven

Fred continued to see Ivy and the days he spent with her turned the world into a better place. He found he could talk to her about everything, opening his heart. What began as desire, turned into need and evolved into love. Talking to her diminished his fears and began to eat into the nightmares he was prone to. The more his need for her grew, the stronger his love became. He still had nightmares; but they weren't as often, and he still drank, but not as often and not as heavily.

Ivy also found she could talk to Fred and revealed things to him that, other than Ruby, no one else knew. She told him how, when she was away with the army, her parents had been killed in a doodlebug attack and how Ruby had looked after her. Also, that like Ruby, she was also an only child and that the two of them, bereft of family, had grown closer and become more like sisters. She joked that Ruby was certainly the big sister in the relationship and watched over Ivy closer than a mother. She even joked that Fred better watch his step with her. Fred already knew that Ruby didn't care for him and treaded very carefully around her so that a wary truce existed between them. Still, he'd joined in with Ivy's joke at her expense.

As the months progressed, they grew closer and closer and as winter approached, they started to look towards Christmas. As an only child himself, his parents expected him to return home for the festive season, even though he'd been away for several years and he wanted to be with Ivy. In his own mind, he'd arrived at a solution and asked her if she'd like to go with him. She'd been reluctant; stating that his parents didn't know her. He countered that it would be a perfect time to meet them. She'd then expressed concern that she couldn't leave Ruby alone. Fred had been ready for this and said didn't Ruby want to spend it with Duncan?

Ruby had been reluctant to discuss the holiday and Ivy conceded he might have a point and that she'd think about it and have a chat with Ruby. Fred was happy about that as he'd already had a chat with Duncan who had raised the subject in his own blunt way and said:

"Are you spending Christmas with Ivy? You like each other and it's a good time to do the deed. Because I take it you haven't. Besides, I want to spend it with Ruby." He winked as he said this and Fred had only nodded his head in mute agreement.

In truth, he hadn't slept with Ivy, as much as he would have liked to. But he wasn't Duncan. In the end, Ivy had agreed to his plan as long as his parents were happy. He'd quickly assured her they would be.

And so, on a chilly Christmas Eve, they stood on the windy platform of the railway station. Fred would have travelled earlier as the school had broken for the holidays several days earlier but Ivy was nervous and didn't want to impose on his parents too long. Besides, she would have had to take additional holidays from work and they were at a premium with those wanting to spend time with their children. The war years had caused too many separations and people were trying to make up for lost time. They caught an early train to avoid the rush and later on sat side by side in an empty compartment. Ivy gripped his hand tightly, nervous about the forthcoming meeting.

"Do you think they'll like me?" she asked.

"They'll love you," he replied, "just like I do." The answer had come spontaneously, he didn't have the guile to charm insincerely. Ivy was surprised, Fred was not a demonstrative type, which was part of his problem, experience and upbringing had forged him into a man who couldn't display weakness and thus who found it difficult to express his feelings. She felt progress was being made.

She snuggled against him. "Thank you, and I love you too." A bridge had been crossed. The rest of the journey passed in peaceful contentment as they rattled across the winter landscape and finally pulled into the small station near Fred's home; a symbol of what would soon be a bygone age: two small platforms facing each other across the tracks with an ornate wrought iron bridge spanning the distance between them. They alighted at the platform on the exit side of the station and passed through an archway between the ticket office and small buffet, Fred walking manfully up the lane towards the main street, carrying both their cases. He was on home ground and wanted Ivy to like it. She walked next to him and could sense his excitement.

"I went to school just over there," he pointed across the road, "it seems to be so long ago but also just like yesterday."

"That's nice. We should remember the good times and forget all the bad times that have happened in between. That's how I cope."

"I'm sorry," he said, "I'm rabbiting on about on about home and forgetting that yours is gone now."

"No, I'm not saying that, I'm glad that you're happy to be home, that you have fond memories from here and I want to share them with you. But I'm frightened of meeting your parents."

"Don't be, they're nice people and I'm sure you'll like them. Anyway, we'll be there soon." Saying that he turned off the high street and led her up the street to his parent's home, noticing that the street had regained its well cared for appearance again. Or, he realised, it could be because he was seeing things differently now. All he'd known before was anger and despair, but now he had hope again and it was a good feeling. Finally, they turned into the garden and walked up the path.

"Here we are." Just as he said that the door opened and his father stood there. "That was quick."

"You're joking," said his father, "'your' mother has been stood at the window for the last half hour watching for you. I told her the time the train was due in but it made no difference. She's been on tenterhooks all morning waiting to meet your girl. If she's dusted that sitting room once, she's done it a hundred times." He turned to Ivy, "So you're the lass who's stolen our lad's heart. And I don't wonder, what's a good-looking girl like you doing with an ugly brute like him?" He playfully ruffled Fred's hair as he said this.

"Oh, he's not so bad," she started to relax, deciding quickly that she liked his father. Despite his jovial manner, she could tell he was an intelligent man. Of medium height, like Fred, he was still slim and fit looking, and well turned out. But by his comfort, she knew that although he may have dressed with care for her visit, he was used to dressing like that and his immaculate shirt testified to his wife's care.

"Well, don't just stand there in the cold. Come on, lad, bring her in and put your mother out of her misery." He stood to one side to let Ivy in the hallway. She saw the long hallway was spotless and, as she was to discover, just like the rest of the house. Its tiled floor was not only washed, but shone with polish. It led straight through to the kitchen and as she looked down, the door from it opened and his mother bustled out. Bustled was the correct word, a small woman, she was full of energy, talking rapidly as she rushed to embrace Fred and, to Ivy's surprise, her as well. Her chatter barely disguised her nervousness.

"Frederick, take those cases upstairs. You're in your old room, Ivy is in the double at the back. Thomas, take the girls coat and take her into the front room, let her get warm. I'll put the kettle on."

"Sunday names, is it," said his father, as his wife shot him a look of admonishment. He hung Ivy's coat on the stand in the hall and led her through to a comfortable sitting room where a fire burned in the grate sending waves of warmth across the room. Everything in the room showed care, pristine nets hanging over the windows flanked by well-hung curtains. Occasional tables and sideboard polished to brilliance, not a mark on the fireplace. But for all that it radiated comfort in a happy house. She heard Fred's footsteps on the stairs moments before he stepped through the door. He sat on the sofa next to Ivy.

"Mother been cleaning again," he said looking around.

"Again, she never stops. And she's been even worse since you said you were bringing Ivy here. I've had to keep moving in case I was polished."

He laughed just as Fred's mother walked into the room.

"A little polish wouldn't do you any harm." The comment carried no malice and Ivy noticed none was taken; they were two people who'd been together a long time and this was something of a game between them. She was carrying a tray loaded with teapot, cups and saucers. "Thomas, make yourself useful and pull a table across."

"Let me help, Mrs Bell," said Ivy jumping up. "Is this okay?" She lifted a table and put it in front of the sofa.

"That's fine, but you shouldn't be doing that, you're a guest." She shot a withering look at Tom, "It's Violet by the way, not Mrs Bell. I'll bring the rest in from the kitchen," she smiled.

"Let me help you, Violet."

"Thank you, dear." She led the way and Ivy followed her into a neat kitchen that, like the rest of house was spotless and neat. On a scrubbed table, by the wall, a number of plates stood stocked with sandwiches and cakes whilst on another wall a dresser displayed beautiful crockery and shiny glasses. It was a workplace but a loved room.

"These," Ivy took a plate of sandwiches and a plate of cakes from the table and carried them through to the sitting room and put them on the table in front of the couch. Violet followed with tea plates and napkins. She poured the tea and they all helped themselves to a sandwich and cake.

"It's not much," said Violet, "but it will keep us going until dinner."

"You're undervaluing yourself, Violet," Ivy said as she ate, "this cake is beautiful. Did you make it?"

"Of course. Do you really like it?" she was pleased and beamed. "Do you cook?"

"Not really, there's not much need. I generally have lunch at work. I used to love to bake with Mum but since she died, I haven't really had the heart. I should get into it again for her sake." Violet looked at her sympathetically.

"It must have been horrible getting that news. Fred told us about it. War is a terrible thing. It's not glorious, it just brings out the worlds wickedness." She glanced at her husband. "That's right, isn't it, Tom?"

"Totally. No man got anything good from it. But that's a depressing topic. Let's talk about something nice. It's not every day your son brings home a pretty girl. Besides its Christmas and a time to be happy." The conversation moved to questions about Ivy and Fred's family. She discovered that Tom was a teacher like Fred and that he was currently the head of a local secondary school. She also learned what a good student Fred had been and how sporty he'd been, playing both rugby and cricket. There was obvious pride when they said this and the afternoon passed pleasantly.

Presently, Tom asked, "What time are we having dinner?" Violet looked at him.

"The usual. Oh no, Thomas Bell, I know what you're up to. You're not dragging Fred off to the pub for your usual pre-prandial." She turned to Ivy, "He does this all the time you know, and he uses the term to disguise the fact that he likes a drink, he's not getting Fred to leave you alone."

"I don't mind, I'm sure Fred and his dad need to catch up. Why don't I help you with dinner and it will give us a chance to chat without them?" She turned to Fred, "Just a quick one mind." He nodded meekly whilst his father laughed.

"She got your measure, boy, but I like her."

"And yours," Violet interrupted. "And so have I so the same goes for you. Don't be all night and get going, you're wasting time."

Still laughing, Tom got his coat and Fred followed him out of the door.

"Do you think they'll do as they're told?" Ivy asked as they left.

"Of course. A quick one will be two and half an hour a full hour but they'll be back for dinner. It's a game we've been playing for years. Tom likes a drink to relax him but he's never been a drunk so I don't deny him. I saw too many come back from the last war scarred and shocked and turning to drink and ruining what was left of their lives. You'd see them on street corners, the worst ones sleeping rough and drinking meths. I know Tom went through hell and I could see the pain in his eyes when he looked at them. What I've always tried to do is make somewhere safe for him to come home to, to have as much normality as I could for him. It nearly destroyed him when Fred went away to war and he fretted every day until he came home and we knew he was safe. We were worried at first because he was so withdrawn. Tom told me to leave him alone and that he would work it out himself. He seems to have and is coping but I know from experience that these things never fully go away. Tom has had nightmares all through our marriage but we just accept them and carry on when they happen. It's why we were so happy when he asked if he could bring you home for Christmas. He's like all men, he needs someone to look after him. Sorry, that doesn't appear very welcoming. Does it?"

"No, the opposite actually. I saw too many young men damaged by the war when I was based in Italy and Fred has told me about his experiences in Burma which, frankly, were horrific. If they're only going to be an hour or so hadn't we better start dinner?"

"No need, everything is done and ready to switch on. There's a bottle of sherry, why don't we have a glass and you can tell me all about Italy, and you can tell me about Fred during the war because he doesn't tell us and we don't press him."

As Violet and Ivy settled down with their sherry, Tom and Fred were entering the lounge bar of the Rose and Crown. This time, there was a cheery fire blazing in the grate and a pleasant warmth permeating the room. It was also fuller and full of good cheer for the festive holiday. Jack, as usual, was behind the bar and greeted them as they came in.

"I see you've got the war hero back with you, what can I get you?" Fred winced at the reference; for him war was not glorious and there were no heroes. Jack didn't notice Fred's expression but his father had.

"Couple of pints please, Jack, and get yourself one." He turned to Fred, "Go find some seats, lad and I'll bring these over." Fred gratefully scanned the room, in his own environment, he would be in control but this was his father's domain and he let him take the lead. In many ways, he reverted to his old relationship with his father when he came home, deferential and obedient.

With other men, he was authoritarian, often to the point of bullishness, but with him, he was mild, trusting him as always to make the right decision. He spotted a table with a couple of chairs near the far corner, away from the bustle nearer the bar where men jovially welcomed the start of the holiday. He settled himself down just as his father approached with their drinks.

"Good choice, son, at least we can hear ourselves here." Fred smiled, it had been there or nowhere, some choice. "Now, you can tell me all about this lass of yours?"

"There's not much to tell you, she's nice and I'm very fond of her."

"I'd say you were a bit more than fond. Now, don't get me wrong, I think she is a lovely girl, but I want you to be sure what you want."

"I want her," spluttered Fred, "she makes me feel calm. When I'm with her, the world seems a better place."

Tom looked at him, "and when you're not, it doesn't? Believe it not, I know exactly what you mean. When I came back from the last war, I was a wreck. I'd seen too much, too much horror and far too much stupidity from those who were running the war but not fighting it or dying in it. Life seemed to have no meaning. But I was lucky, I had your mother and she was there like a rock for me, an anchor against the storm and the nightmares I had for years. So, then things improved, or at least I could learn to live with the memories. And I've tried to live a normal life, enjoying the better things, and that's what you must do. If this girl is what it takes, go ahead with my blessing. We've only got one life and you've still got yours. So live it."

Fred had never heard his father speak that way before; when it came to the war, he was usually reticent to the point of silence but now Fred understood where he was coming from and felt closer to him because of it and less alone himself.

"I will do, thanks for telling me that. Now how many drinks can we get away with before we go home?" He smiled.

Chapter Twenty-Eight

It was, fortunately, a warm day in what had been an unseasonably wet June when they gathered at the small Norman Church on the approach to the city. Its' squat towered structure, dating back nine hundred years, nestled in the old, but not quite as ancient, homes jumbled around it. It was the parish church where Ivy shared a house with Ruby and the obvious choice for the wedding. It also had a warm comforting feel about it and a picturesque interior, with glorious stained-glass windows at its west end illuminating the altar and small choir. The war could not damage what the years had failed to do and the church stood as a testament to solidity and continuity. A perfect setting for a wedding.

Fred stood outside the door with Duncan by his side. Ruby was Ivy's obvious choice as maid of honour and, not to be left out, Duncan had appointed himself as best man. Fred had been torn between Duncan and Alex but the matter had been taken out of hands. As Ivy had no parents and close male relatives, Alex had agreed to give her away so all the friends were part of the day. It was to be a small affair, just the close friends and Fred's parents. Tom had taken an instant dislike to Duncan ignoring Fred's defence of his friend.

As he put it bluntly, "He's your friend and that's your choice, but he is what he is." About Ruby, he was as scathing, "Look, son, I think the world of Ivy but that friend of hers is very pretty but a sour bugger." And that was where the argument ended. But this was Fred and Ivy's day and everybody was going to do their best to make it perfect.

"Do you think she'll turn up?" asked Fred as he and Duncan lit yet another cigarette as they paced up and down, much to Duncan's frustration as he tried to calm the agitated groom down. The church already contained a sprinkling of people who had come to witness the ceremony; colleagues of Fred's from school and a few from Ivy's office. A couple of old school friends of Ivy's had also travelled up with their husbands. There would have been more guests had either of them wanted the ceremony in their home towns, as Ivy couldn't bear the thought without her parents and Fred was not callous to ignore her feelings. Besides, the city was where they had made their home.

"Of course, she'll turn up although if she's as nervous as you, God help us." He saw the look of concern on Fred's face as he said this and regretted his words. "Look, she's with Ruby and Alex, do you think either of them would let anything go wrong. Blimey, I wish we'd had that drink before, I could certainly use it now."

"So could I, but like I told you I promised Ivy I wouldn't and I won't break that promise." Duncan didn't agree; promises were made to be broken as far as he was concerned. But he knew there was no point in arguing with Fred; he could usually persuade him to do things but where Ivy was concerned, he was intractable. At that point, however, they were distracted as they saw the car pull up at the end of the cottages flanking the church forming a corridor to the church gate.

"Quick, my boy, let's get you inside. It won't look good if the bride turns up and there's no one waiting for her. Besides, it's unlucky to see the bride before she stands beside you." This last was said as he saw Fred craning to see if Ivy was in the car. He hustled Fred into the church, between the pews and up to the altar, nodding to Fred's parents as he passed, reassuring them everything was okay.

Violet smiled, but Tom remained stiff lipped. A ripple passed through the congregation in anticipation as Duncan settled the groom into his place. A commotion at the door preceded the organ striking up the wedding march announcing the bride's arrival. Fred and Duncan turned to see Ivy, holding on to Alex, walking towards them. Ruby walked demurely behind them although to Fred it looked like she was more riding shotgun. But as he looked, Ivy took his breath away. Clothing rationing had lifted, but the new fashion was for less rather than more and Ivy wore a tea length dress which was not only economical but showed off her figure. Fred couldn't believe it as she glided towards him. He would like to say later that it was his happy day; which it was, but in truth, he would later remember very little about it. He had a vague recollection of muttering responses when prodded, but the rest was lost in a sea of happy bewilderment.

Before Fred realised it, they had reached the end of the ceremony and he found himself walking back down the aisle with his new bride on his arm. At the front of the church, the congregation had gathered to shower them with confetti as they posed for the obligatory photograph on the steps. After they had received the good wishes of friends and thanked them for coming, they left for the wedding tea. As this was in one of the better hotels in the city, and only a short way from the church, they had decided to walk to the venue.

The small party set off heading down to the city, walking past Fred's old college and down the hill to the river. An old wrought iron footbridge spanned the river and took them to the south bank and a short, pleasant walk along the riverside led them into the hotel. The dining room was resplendent with its starched linen and floral arrangements, illuminated from the sunlight streaming in through the large picture windows.

Although rationing was easing, they had kept the menu simple and only catered for a small party; Fred's parents, the friends who had travelled for the day and of course, Duncan, Ruby and Alex. They sat at a single, long table that allowed for easy conversation and removed the need for formal speeches although Duncan still stood to propose a toast to the bride and groom with the whisky and sherry provided. The rest of the meal was more in the manner of a high tea; with tea being the main beverage on offer, to accompany the cold meat salad, scones and selection of cakes. But in those early post war years, it seemed a treat. There was no post meal party and towards the early evening, the guests began to drift away with Fred and Ivy the first to leave as a taxi arrived to take them away.

The couple had not planned a honeymoon; austerity had yet to end and they had, in any case, sunk all their savings into buying a house of their own. On Alex's advice, they had bought a house in the village on the outskirts of the city where he lived. It was still convenient for the city and also close to Fred's school, and, as Alex had assured them, was certain to be developed and a good investment. Ivy had immediately fallen in love with the property, a double fronted stone built Victorian semi-detached with a large garden and views to the Church at the front.

With its high street offering a selection of small grocers, chapels and public houses it had a tight community feel and she had felt settled for the first time since her parents had died and her old home was lost to her. There was work to do, but they were young and fit and up to the challenge. Ivy wanted a home and somewhere to provide Fred with the stability he needed. That stability also included Alex who was nearby and who could always provide a calming influenced on Fred, unlike Duncan who was a total party animal and womaniser. Ivy was well aware of his reputation and was sure Ruby was as well. She didn't know why Ruby tolerated his behaviour but she believed he was like a naughty child and Ruby loved him like a forgiving mother.

Ivy was reminded of Duncan as Fred, with bravado, opened the front door and, lifting her, carried her over the threshold. On the stand in the hall stood a bottle of champagne from him; where he had got it was no one's business and with Duncan you didn't ask questions. But it was a nice touch and she was moved. Deep down, he had a lovely side, it just didn't surface very often. She often wondered what he was hiding and what had happened to make him that way.

Fred interrupted her thoughts, "Are we going to drink that, Mrs Bell?" She laughed and agreed it seemed like a good idea. They took the bottle into the kitchen, the house was a work in progress and only the kitchen, bedroom and bathroom were finished and decorated: somewhere to cook, eat sleep and wash. They took glasses from the kitchen cupboard and sat either side of the small kitchen table. As they raised a toast Fred looked at her.

"This isn't very comfortable, is it?" he said, "Why don't we take the bottle upstairs?"

Ivy felt shy. During their courtship, she had not slept with Fred and he hadn't pressed. In fact, she had not slept with anyone; during her army days Ruby had fended off all the young officers that had passed through the office and she'd had no sweetheart to come home to.

"Okay," she said. Together, they walked up the stairs to start their married life.

Chapter Twenty-Nine

Married life began well for Fred and Ivy; Ivy was content planning and renovating the house and Fred was still feeling euphoric at his new status. An added bonus was that his more relaxed attitude improved his relationship with his colleagues. An added delight was the pleasure they both found in the physical side of their marriage; after a shy start for both of them passion increased and with it, contentment. Fred's drinking came more under control; he still saw Alex every Tuesday in the local and Friday in the city when Duncan would join them. If, rarely, he felt the need for a drink, on other days he became what was known as a last orders man, popping out for a quick one at 10 o'clock before time was called. Ivy was happy with his behaviour and his attention and devotion to her. That was until the nightmares began.

It seemed that the more Fred became content, the more the past came back to haunt him. The first time it occurred, Ivy was awakened by Fred screaming and tossing in the bed next to her. As she'd leaned across to him, she'd seen that he was still asleep. Not knowing what to do, she'd awakened him, sweaty and wild-eyed, he'd taken time to calm down and had then fallen asleep with his arm draped around her. She'd seen enough shell-shocked men during her time in Italy but that had occurred during conflict and she was unprepared for the event now.

It would be many years before the causes of post-traumatic stress were recognised, but then it was left to the individual and his family to deal with it. Ivy had thought they would talk about it the following morning after Fred had more settled sleep but in the morning, he was reluctant to talk about it and actually clammed up when she questioned him. She was at a loss about how to deal with it whereas Fred, who was apparently used to such events, retreated to the pub that night.

The following day, he was full of remorse and apologises but still reluctant to talk about what had happened. A pattern began to emerge with his behaviour; for weeks he would be okay and then the nightmares would return and he would be thrashing in bed and awakening wild eyed. These episodes always came after Fred became stressed; or more accurately, angry at someone. She could comfort him when he woke but couldn't get him to talk and was at a loss how to deal with the effects. In desperation, she turned to Alex who; more than anyone else, acted as Fred's conscious.

Alex was a constant in Fred and Ivy's life. It was him who had helped them find the house and advised them when they'd decided to buy. He lived only a short walk away along the high street in his father's old house. Although he lived close by and was a fairly frequent visitor, she had never been to his house before. However, she needed his advice and could only ask him when Fred wasn't present so she found herself walking down the high street one night when she knew Fred had a late staff meeting and knocking on his door.

Alex answered the door and seemed surprised to see her standing there. Quickly, she said she needed to talk to him about Fred and he reluctantly invited her in. She was both confused and a little hurt by his attitude but overlooked this because of her need for help. As he led her into the sitting room, he casually turned a framed photograph he had obviously been looking at facedown onto the small table next to his chair. Ivy took in her surroundings as he did this.

Alex's father had been a widower and had lived a bachelor's life for many years and it seemed Alex was following suit. The house was spotless but austere, clearly lacking a woman's touch and the softness it would have brought to turn the house into a home. The sitting room was more a scholar's study, full of books and papers. She seated herself in a chair he indicated opposite him. His demeanour now changed to one of concern as he looked at her.

"Now, Ivy, what's troubling you?" As he said this, Ivy felt the tears coming. She told him about Fred's nightmares, how he turned to drink when it happened and how he wouldn't talk to her about it. The more she talked, the more the tears came and it finished with Alex kneeling in front of her, holding her hands as he tried to reassure her.

Finally, he said, "I know it's awful for the pair of you, for Fred suffering like this and for you having to watch and feel so helpless to do anything about it. But take my word for this, it has nothing to do with anything you've done. Fred tells me repeatedly that you're the best thing that has ever happened to him, in a way you've saved him and continue to do so. The nightmares will pass but it will take time. You may not know it but Fred was in one of the bloodiest conflicts of the war and in the worst part of it. It hasn't been called the forgotten war for nothing, we've all heard about the prisoners the Japanese took but not much about the men who fought them."

Ivy listened, both fascinated and horrified, as Alex told her how Fred, and other selected men, had been dropped in the jungle and played cat and mouse guerrilla warfare with the enemy for years, being chased between sharp and bloody bouts of hand to hand combat during which he saw his best friend slaughtered. How, at the end, he'd been part of the horror of Imphal where they'd slaughtered the Japanese in their thousands.

She'd told him that Fred had told her some things about it but he would not talk about the war. To that Alex explained that few men would, that the horror of it all was bad enough but for men like Fred, men who'd witnessed events such as Imphal, there was also a sense of regret and shame at what they'd been obliged to do. Ivy could only nod as he spoke with the tears falling gently down her cheeks.

Finally, Alex stood, "I'll go make some tea, unless you'd like something stronger. I've only got whisky I'm afraid." She told him tea would be fine and he left to the kitchen.

Ivy was left alone in the room with her thoughts. No wonder Fred had nightmares. She stood to stretch her shoulders and back after sitting hunched for so long and wandered around the room. Finally, her eyes rested on the table where the photograph still lay face down where Alex had left it. Idly, she turned it over and lifted it to get a closer look at the image. She was surprised to see it portrayed a beautiful dark-haired woman. As she looked closer, she saw it was inscribed with the message *to my beloved Alex – Helene*. She stood transfixed looking at the woman as Alex returned with a tray bearing a teapot and cups.

She didn't know what to say and blurted out, "I'm sorry, I didn't mean to pry."

Looking at the horror on her face, Alex said, "It's all right, I shouldn't have left it out."

"No, it's your house, you shouldn't have to worry about people picking things up. She's a beautiful woman and a bit exotic, if you don't mind me saying. An old girlfriend?"

"She was half French, and no, she wasn't an ex-girlfriend, she was my wife." Ivy was taken aback, unable to ask further until she looked at Alex's face and saw the absolute despair on it. Finally, she found her tongue.

"I didn't know you were married?" Ruby certainly didn't know or she would never have introduced them. Alex must have read her mind.

"I'm not, she died during the war."

"Not another blitz victim. That's how I lost my parents, you remember. Too many went that way."

"Would that she had, it would have been kinder that way." Ivy was surprised by his answer, why would being blown up be a preferable way of dying. She looked at the sadness in his eyes and clasped his hands. Alex didn't pull away but gripped her hands in return even as his head bowed, him seated and she kneeling on the floor by him. He could tell she needed further explanation. "She was shot in France by the Germans." Ivy was trying to grasp the implications of this.

"She was living there during the war?"

"No, she was there in the run up to D Day liaising with the resistance." Now, Ivy was both amazed and confused. She'd heard about such missions during her own time in the forces but had never met anyone involved. Also, she wondered how Alex had met her.

"How did you two meet?"

"I was her controller. We married after she returned from what should have been her last mission. I should never have

145

let her go again. But in war, what choice do we have." Ivy looked at him closely: it was bad enough to lose someone, and so tragically as well, and how must you feel if it was you who sent them to their death. The agony the man must be feeling was incomprehensible, she realised that none of them really knew Alex at all. He was always there for all of them, the shoulder they all leaned on unaware of the personal demons he was hiding.

She wished to console him, to let him know he wasn't alone, that he wasn't to blame. She placed her hands on the side of his head and pulled him close, he responded clinging tight to her and shaking. She didn't know how it happened, but she found herself kissing him and responding.

Later, she lay next to him in his bed. Strangely, she didn't feel any guilt, he'd clung to her desperately during their lovemaking and cried after. But now he lay calm, back in control of himself.

"You came to see me about Fred, not to get involved in my problems. Some friend I am, as well as being a lousy husband."

"You're not a bad friend, nor were you a lousy husband. You're just damaged like the rest of us. We all need each other and we'll always be here for one another. But this must never happen again."

He knew she was right, here was a girl for him but he could never have her. But he could look after her.

"You're right. I'll have a word with Fred, everything will be all right again."

Chapter Thirty

Fred met Alex for their usual Tuesday night drink. Alex had been as good as his word and had talked, and more importantly, listened to Fred over the last few months. At first, Fred had been reticent about his problems, but as he'd opened up, it was as if a dam had burst and even Alex had been amazed by the things Fred had been holding in and the issues that had developed. But the more he'd talked, the more composed he'd become.

Alex realised that, as well as memories of traumatic events, Fred was also carrying a lot of personal guilt. Alex had spent a lot of time convincing him that whatever had happened wasn't his fault which had seemed to comfort him. He still had occasional bad dreams but he could now control the after affects and get on with his life. He'd been a lot better following that but this evening he was in particular high spirits, joking with the regulars and generally being the life and soul of the party.

"You seem to have come out of yourself young man," Alex joked.

"With good reason. By the way, I never thanked you properly for listening to my moaning and wittering on. You could have done without that, but don't think I don't appreciate it."

"You're welcome, what are friends for. But come on, what's got you so cheerful."

Fred beamed and took his friend by the shoulder to whisper, "I'm going to be a father." Alex hadn't expected that nor the joy on his friend's face. He forced a reply.

"That's great news. You're obviously over the moon. How is Ivy, is she happy?"

"Of course, she is. It's what we both want. She was a bit unsure at first but that's only natural. As she said, it's a bit scary for a woman but now we're planning and everything is great."

"So, when's the happy event?"

"Not for ages yet, she's only a few months. So, we're keeping things pretty quiet for the moment." Alex's head was spinning as he did rapid mental calculations.

"So, who else have you told?"

"Only you, and there's a reason for this. We'd like you to be the child's godfather." Alex was now in total confusion.

"Is Ivy okay with that?"

"Of course. She thinks it's a good idea, she likes you, thinks you're a good influence on me. The only thing we disagreed on was names. I said if it was a boy, I would like to call him Alex, after you. But she said if it was a boy, she wanted to call him Christopher after her father. You don't mind, do you?"

That would have been too much, thought Alex.

"Quite right too. Anyway, you might have a girl." He thought quickly, he knew Ivy loved Fred and wanted to be with him. He wasn't going to spoil that, and anyway, he wasn't certain of anything. But he could still be part of the child's life regardless. "I'd be proud to be the child's godfather."

Fred put his arm around his shoulder. "Great, let's have a drink to celebrate."

Chapter Thirty-One

Bob shivered on the platform of the colliery station as he began the first stage of his long journey to, what he believed was, misery. He would change trains at the main station for the longer part of his journey. In his pocket, he had his Enlistment Notice and travel warrant which had arrived by post together with a postal order for four shillings. He was bemused by that until he discovered that it represented a day's pay for a National Serviceman and that on the day he travelled on the warrant, he was officially in the army.

Although he knew that one day he would be called up, he lived in the forlorn hope, like thousands of others, that he would be overlooked or that the practice would be abandoned before he was due to be called. It would be several years later that the practice was abandoned and his first thought when it was announced was for the lucky bastards who'd missed it.

National Service had not featured in any of Bob's plans. He was one of the lucky ones who'd passed for the grammar school and his father, pressurised by his mother, had agreed he could attend. His father was rooted in the colliery life and saw little value in what he called 'fancy ideas'. But even at an early age, Bob had no desire to follow his father and contemporaries 'down the pit'. So, at eleven and in the uniform begrudgingly bought by his father, he started his secondary education.

He was a clever boy and did well in his studies. But he knew that university was never going to be an option for him and saw no point therefore in entering the sixth form. With no desire to remain long term in the village, he looked wider for employment. As it happened, one of the national chain stores was recruiting trainees for its local stores and, armed with glowing references from his headmaster he had applied and been accepted to train at the nearest store in the old city.

His father had been scathing considering that it was not the job for a man, exclaiming the 'money's crap' and 'how's a man supposed to keep a wife and kids on it.' The gulf between his father and him had been growing for years and had reached the point where Bob had little time for him. He knew the pay, at first, was considerably less than he could earn manually but he had ambition. So, on the first chilly morning, he had left very early to get the bus into the old city. It was early but his father had scathingly said he 'didn't know what early was and he should he should try pit shifts'. Bob had bit his tongue and not retorted 'that that was the whole point', and he never intended working shifts.

Bob had, like all trainees, rotated around the departments, and tackled every task given to him with enthusiasm, but it was in the accounts department that he really started finding his feet. After work, he started night classes in bookkeeping at the technical college in the city. Not only did he enjoy the classes but he found himself with other young men keen to advance and received assurance that he was doing the right thing.

After years of fighting the trend at home and in the village, he felt comfortable and didn't begrudge the fact that on college nights he arrived home late, riding the empty bus passing brightly lit houses and pubs. His confidence was growing and he was becoming settled. He was also growing physically and the girls at work were starting to notice him.

The girls back in the village, the daughters of miners, were only interested in the lads working there with the tradesmen being the cream of the crop. But the company had been recruiting the brighter girls from the secondary schools who wanted a different future. Bob had decided he didn't want any long-term girlfriend at that stage; he had no intention of being tied down. However, all in all he was happy.

That happiness was shattered when his call up papers turned up: they were rare in the village where most of the young men were in an exempt industry and the odd professional's sons had university deferment. His manager was sympathetic having served in the last war and advised him to 'get some in' and then come back to work. He told him he was well thought of which in Bob's case was true; he'd already been noticed and considered someone to watch for the future provided he continued to work like he'd been doing. Reassured that he'd have a job waiting for him on his return he decided to bite the bullet and 'do his bit'.

Which was why he now found himself on the windy platform heading into the unknown. Somebody must have shown some initiative; or it could just have been a coincidence, but given his background, had posted him to the Royal Army Pay Corps with instructions to report to their training centre at Devises in Wiltshire. Bob, like the rest of the children in his village, had never been further than the club trip to Redcar or Whitley Bay and, despite his apprehension, was enjoying the experience of travelling, even though the carriage on the train proved to be uncomfortable as the train rattled down the rails.

After what seemed an eternity, he arrived at Devises where he found the station staff well used to greeting young and confused adolescents clutching suitcases with their worldly possessions and reminders of home. Directed to a bus that would take him to the barracks, he eventually arrived at the forbidding camp where he would spend the next ten weeks of his life. Within hours of arrival, all the recruits had been shaved, hairs cut and kitted out so that they all looked identical. Only in the barrack room did any individuality survive and Bob was surprised at the number of boys who cried themselves to sleep at night. They were all young but he was surprised that it wasn't the posh public schoolboys but the hard-working class lads who were in tears after lights out.

The public schoolboys had been way from home from the age of seven and they had already done their crying for their mothers. The tough lads from the factories whose mums made their teas, washed their clothes and made their beds found National Service hard. Overnight, they had to learn a new language. 'Blanco', 'spit and polish', 'rifle oil', 'pull throughs' and the dreaded 'bull and jankers'.

But the arena for breaking these young men was the parade ground. In squads, the boys learnt to obey orders instinctively, and to react to a single word of command, by coping with a torrent of abuse from the drill sergeants. Bruce Kent, leader of CND, later recollected that he found his sergeants demented psychopaths who positively enjoyed shouting at and insulting new recruits. Bob couldn't agree more.

In addition, failure on the parade ground led to punishments which ranged from the tedious such as peeling spuds to the totally mindless such as painting coal white, cleaning the parade ground with a toothbrush or scraping the barracks floor with a razor blade. Also, there was no time to yourself. Every waking moment was filled with polishing, parading, running, jumping, climbing, polishing, eating and more polishing. Bob found the regime pointless and demeaning but saw the wisdom in not arguing.

But what Bob found truly galling was that despite having to go into uniform, being barked at by sadistic NCOs was the fact they were paid a measly four shillings a day for the privilege. Despite his father's contempt, Bob was used to earning his own wage and the independence it gave him. He truly resented what he considered was going back onto pocket money. But he knew he had no choice but to comply; the army, government and society were in support of it and to walk away meant prison, which was how he considered this and, like prison, he decided to do his time and as the popular opinion amongst his contemporaries was 'get some in and then get out.'

Things improved with posting. Bob's intake was lucky to have been conscripted after Korea and were in no danger of being sent to that war-ravaged country. Conflicts still flared across the old colonial empire but the regiment to which he was attached wasn't called to serve there, nor in the army on the Rhine and he spent his service in dismal garrison towns away from danger. Bob was also fortunate in that his immediate superior was a regular approaching the end of his service and both lazy and incompetent.

Like many men in his position, he tried to bully his subordinates but Bob had kept his head down and complied with every command. An understanding developed between him and his sergeant that he could be relied upon and therefore was best left alone. The final turning point came when a spot check occurred and a discrepancy was found in the accounts.

As Sergeant Blake went into major meltdown, worrying about his position and pension, Bob had calmly asked if he could look at the problem. With the skills developed at work and night school, he had quickly spotted the error in the accounts which he quickly corrected. Having no desire to progress in the army; he had deliberately chosen, as a grammar school boy, not to apply for a short service commission, knowing that for someone who despised the army as he did, it was not a good choice. He merely wanted to do his time as easily as he could and then get back to his life.

So, instead of making it known he had corrected the problem he had gone to Blake, shown him the problem, explained how he had corrected it and left it to him to go to their superiors and let them know the issue had been dealt with. He was in no doubt that Blake would take the credit but that was his intention. Blake returned with a grin like the proverbial Cheshire cat and as he passed Bob's desk paused, and laying his hand on his shoulder said, "Thanks, lad."

From that point on, their relationship changed as Bob took on more and more of the responsibilities of the office and Blake took more of a backseat. Bob didn't mind; if he had to work there he would rather run things his way and if he got an easy ride all the better. As part of this, he volunteered for every course that was available which Blake was happy to endorse. If he had to be there he was going to get something out of it.

Time started to pass more pleasantly and he became the de facto leader of the office. The other clerks began to approach him with their problems so he became a conduit between them and the sergeant. He was able to resolve things for them and became popular.

What he was doing did not go unnoticed and near the end of his service he was approached by the sergeant major who asked, "Have you thought what you're going to do next?"

Bob thought carefully before replying, "Going back to get on with my life sergeant major."

"You could make a life here you know. Sergeant Blake is retiring soon. If you signed on as a regular, you would get stripes. It's not a bad life."

"Thanks," he didn't wish to cause offence, "but I have other plans."

"A girl, is it?"

"Yes," he lied. It was easier than arguing.

"Well, good luck then." He shook his hand. "If you change your mind, come and see me."

Chapter Thirty-Two

Bob didn't change his mind, there was never any danger of that occurring. But if there was anything the army had taught him it was not to rock the boat. Smiling sweetly, he said goodbye to Blake who seemed genuinely sorry to see him go and had asked him, "Drop me a line, son, to let me know how you're getting on."

He'd promised he would even though he had no intention of doing so and had left with only one regret that the army had taken two years of his life when he had other plans. Other than that, he had boarded the train home dressed as a civilian once more. He also had money in his pocket; he'd had savings before he was conscripted and he'd not had to open a post office account as dictated by the army. He'd also been parsimonious during his service, a non-smoker and moderate drinker he'd spent most of his time studying determined to pick up where he'd left off. So in a good suit, with money in his wallet he'd set off, a civilian once more and determined never to put himself at the beck and call of anyone else again.

Stepping off the train the village looked the same only smaller and shabbier. A wind was blowing across the platform as it had been when he'd left and he thought nothing's changed as he pulled his coat around himself and lifted his case. He hadn't been home since joining up; there'd been little point. It was a long journey and he'd never felt homesick apart from how he put it 'sick of his home'. But he needed to come home so he could get back to work: he'd written to the company who'd confirmed his job was open for him and they'd be happy to see him. So he'd bitten the proverbial bullet and come back to the village.

Toting his case, he walked the terraced streets heavy with the smell of coal smoke: a miner's fire never went out. It had been raining earlier making the air heavier and the streets glistened. The church stood on the corner, solid and uncompromising. A lot like the place itself he thought. And added to himself and 'what a depressing hole'. Still, he wouldn't be here forever and that thought cheered him.

Many years' later, people would ask him if he ever went back and he would answer honestly 'only when I'm depressed, it cheers me up when I drive out and realise I'll never have to live there again'. Further along the numbered terraces: the colliery had never bothered to name them and it amused him to think of the unfortunate family that lived in Thirteen Thirteenth Street, he saw his parent's house, indistinguishable from all the others apart from the pristine net curtains hanging at the window.

His mother took great pride in the appearance of the house and what it lacked in grandeur it made up for in cleanliness. He often felt sorry for his mother and wondered why she had married his father. She spent what little spare time she had in the local church whereas he was happy in the local club or on his allotment with the other men. It was as if she'd married him because she had no other choice in the small community and there was no other avenue open to her. In many ways, she'd unwittingly influenced his thinking; she'd been trapped and he was determined not to be kept here.

He walked around the end of the terrace and down the back lane; no one used the front doors much and the kitchen was where they lived during the day. High walls surrounded the yards to each house whose flagged floors were barren and provided access to the lavatory and coalhouse. There was no garden, the rear was utilitarian and the front opened onto the street. Only the deputies' houses had front gardens with similar back yards to the rest.

As he clicked the latch on the yard gate his mother came to the kitchen door. He'd written that he'd be home today; he couldn't ring because no one in the village had a telephone and, even if they did there was no one to ring as children rarely left the community and it had reached the situation that, in some way, everybody was related to everyone else. When someone did rarely move away, they would ring the call box on the corner from a call box from where they were at a prearranged time. The recipient would loiter by the box waiting for the telephone to ring. Everyone would know what was happening and it was quite common for the person leaving the box to be greeted by a passer-by with the words 'how's your Ethel/Joan' etc. It would rarely be a man's name; men didn't call.

"You're home," she said as she embraced him on the step. He hadn't been home since he'd been conscripted, but he had written to his mother fairly regularly to let her know he was all right. She must have been waiting for him knowing what time the train was due, "The kettles on and I've been baking." He smiled, if there was anything he missed about home it was her cooking; she was renowned for her cakes and pastry. "Your father is due in from shift shortly, take your case upstairs and I'll make some tea, your rooms ready for you."

He smiled wryly, pecked her on the cheek and picked his case back up. He was not looking forward to seeing his father and the inevitable sarcasm that would occur but it was something that would have to be endured for the time being. Resignedly he carried the case up the narrow stairs that led up from the front door, being careful not to catch the walls as he went. His room was just as he'd left it but spotless as always; it was if his mother had maintained it as a shrine and he felt a momentary pang of guilt. He put the case on the bed; he could unpack later.

Back in the kitchen, his mother said, "I'll pour some tea. We'll eat when your father gets in but you can have a cake to keep you going." He was transported back to his schooldays when he would sit at the table with a cup of tea and a scone, doing his homework and waiting for his father to come in so they could eat dinner. He'd preferred it when his father was on shift and just his mother and he had dinner and he could remain at the table to do his schoolwork in the warmth of the kitchen rather than retreating to his bedroom. He realised his mother missed that too and that she had little company these days.

Placing the cup and plate in front of him, she asked, "And now you can tell me all about the army, what was it like, did you behave and what you are planning now? Your letters weren't very chatty." They weren't, they'd been written out of a sense of duty and therefore short.

"There's not much to tell, it was mainly boring but considering what some of the other lads went through I can't complain about that. And I was lucky that I fell into a job that suited me and gave me an easy ride. As for the rest, there is little to tell, we didn't get paid much and didn't travel. To be honest I spent most of my spare time on courses, the army took two years out of my life and I'm not letting that spoil my plans."

"So, you didn't meet any nice girls while you were away. What are your plans? You said you were going back to work have you agreed a date?" The words came tumbling out, a million questions contained in one sentence and he felt guilty that he hadn't shared his dreams with her but as those dreams involved escape from his home; and thus her, he had been unable to say because he didn't want to hurt her. He answered her in the manner she questioned him.

"No, I didn't meet any nice girls while I was away. My plans are to pick up where I left off and so I'm going back to work on Monday."

"So quick, you're not going to take some time off before you start?" He didn't like to say that there was no point, there was nothing at home to keep him. Instead he was diplomatic.

"The company was good enough to take me back so it's only fair that I don't mess them about. It's also not fair that I hang about here under your feet."

"You're not under my feet, we haven't seen you for so long. It would be nice to spend some time together." *I'm sure father agrees with you,* he thought. As if on cue, the kitchen door opened and his father stepped through, face red from the showers. Without speaking, he hung his coat behind the door and dropped his lunch bag on the sink side. Finally, he spoke.

"I see you're home then. Are you staying this time?" *Straight to the point,* he thought. *No, we'll keep a welcome in the hillsides, no nice to see you. I see you're back, how long are you staying and when are you going.*

"Yes, I'm going back to work on Monday so I'll be here for a while."

"If you can call it work. Don't think you can treat this place as a hotel. It's time you found a lass and got married." Turning to his wife, he said, "I'm meeting Bobby for a quick pint, I'll be back for my dinner." With that he collected his coat and went back out. His mother looked at him but said nothing. *Welcome home,* he thought.

Chapter Thirty-Three

True to his word, Bob returned to work on the Monday morning. As the bus headed for the city, passing through the surrounding villages, his mood lifted as the familiarity of the journey brought back the past and the isolation of the past two years fell away. He felt he was back where he belonged and where he wanted to be. In years to come; no matter where he travelled, as soon as the train pulled into the railway station and he looked across the city, he knew he was home.

The village never was, and never would be home, but the city always would be. He'd walked across the medieval market place to the store and took a deep breath as he entered the building, drawing in the familiar smells of the clothes and other goods. The manager had greeted him and shown him to his desk telling him it was good to have him back and that he'd been missed. There were new faces around, but enough of the old staff to help him settle in.

After a week, Bob felt he'd never been away as he picked up the threads of his old life. This included his thirst for advancement and the long conversation he had with his manager who recognised his thirst and encouraged him as he sought out courses to compliment the experience he already had. Quickly, he slipped back into his old regime of night school after work, followed by a drink in the city with his fellow students before the late bus home.

He had no social life in the village and no desire to be there apart from the fact he needed somewhere to live, or more pertinently to sleep. It also meant he saw little of his father which suited them both. When they did bump into each other, caustic comments were made such as 'good of you to show up' or even worse 'you treat this place like a hotel'.

Bob couldn't argue as it was true so he let the comments pass. Besides, he was there as little as he could be. On his days off, he went into the city, usually going for a swim so he could get a decent shower. In the army, he'd got used to regular showers and the bathing facilities at home were rudimentary at best. All in all, he was seldom at home, and when he was he was generally in his room engrossed in his studies.

His lifestyle actually stood him in good stead at work. Except where his studies coincided, he was always willing to work extra hours and willingly took on any extra tasks that were requested. He had no personal commitments and besides he enjoyed his work. He was appreciated which contrasted with his father's and contemporary's opinion in the village and he rapidly became a company man. But he didn't forget the lessons of the army and how it was best to not to rock the boat. He never complained to his seniors and always had a friendly and helpful word for his colleagues.

As such, whilst he had no close friends, he was well liked and content as such. The girls in the store also began to pay more attention to him but he had no intention of settling down and politely kept his distance. If anything, this made him more of an attraction. But he was career orientated and with the continued approval of his seniors, began moving up the hierarchy of the store. By his early twenties, he was on the management ladder and his earnings increased accordingly. But he didn't waste his money, apart from an occasional social drink he was no boozer and was virulently anti-gambling. His appearance was important but with a generous staff discount, he furnished his wardrobe well.

His father commented, "You buy more clothes than a woman," but bit his tongue when he brought him clothes at discount. He also looked after his mother who proudly went out in her new coats bragging that her clever son had bought them. His standing in the village grew and mothers began telling their daughters that he was a man on the make and a good catch. But he wasn't interested in the local girls, no matter how good looking they were; looks didn't last and he wasn't going to get trapped into a loveless marriage. There was also no way he was going to stay in the village, with

Sunday dinner with the in-laws and a pint in the club before. If he married, he would be gone like a shot.

Chapter Thirty-Four

The years passed. Now, in his early twenties and with the dawn of a new decade he was a rising star in the company and on the management ladder. He was still committed to the company, or rather he was committed to the vehicle that would get him where he wanted to be. He still lived at home but apart from sleeping and the occasional meal was seldom there which fuelled his father's argument that he treated the place like a hotel. However, it was now summer and he had no classes at college as the term had ended and nothing that night to keep him at work so he wound his way down to the bus station to get an earlier bus home; somewhat at a loss what to do with the evening.

As he got to the stand, he saw one of the young girls from work. He didn't usually pay much attention to the girls; he had dates with some of the girls from college but had studiously avoided any involvement at work. But he'd seen this girl before; in the city late one evening he'd seen her out with the other girls and been struck by her. Small, petite and with dark piled hair she was his type. She'd been laughing and joking and was obviously the centre of attention. But he'd forgotten about the attraction until now when he saw her standing here.

"Hello, its Joan, isn't it, what are you doing here?" Realising his gaff, he added quickly, "And don't say waiting for a bus." She laughed, more at his embarrassment than any joke.

"Going the same place as you Mr Lee. Don't you know we live in the same village?" He didn't but then again he had no real social life there.

"No, I didn't. I saw you out with the girls the other night and assumed you lived in the city. By the way, we're not at work so it's Robert, or Robbie if you prefer." He was still young enough to be uncomfortable with the title Mr and it would be years until he became Bob. At the moment, he liked his full name or Robbie as it was trendier.

"Robbie, I like that, it suits you. No, I was out with the girls for my birthday. It was my eighteenth so they took me for a drink."

"Didn't you have a party at home?" he asked. His curiosity was aroused. He couldn't see her out in the village. She seemed to fit in about as much as he did.

"You're joking. Apart from anything else, where would I go? Can you imagine me walking into the miners club and asking for a babycham?" It was his turn to laugh because he could imagine it and the reaction it would provoke. More accurately the outrage.

"You're wrong, I can imagine it. It would cause even more outrage than if I walked in." She giggled and he found he liked the sound. "We've got a problem," he added. "I think we missed he bus and the next one isn't for another half hour. There's a decent coffee house down the road, why don't you let me buy you a coffee and a cake for your birthday?"

"Okay, why not."

They walked together from the station along the street to the Italian coffee house set in the old buildings. It was common of the type that at the time were beginning to replace the more traditional teashops. It was relatively quiet with just a few commuters killing time before their journey home and a couple of shoppers weary from the day. It would be a while before boys met their girlfriends before going to the cinema or older courting couples stole an hour together. They found a quiet corner and he ordered coffees and the promised cakes which arrived in oval glass cups and saucers frothy with milk.

"Tell me, how did you know we lived in the same village?" It hadn't occurred to him that anyone else would be making the same decisions as himself to escape, that he wasn't alone in resenting the stifling environment.

"Oh, all the girls know about you, although," she paused, "their never quite sure what to make of you." Seeing his perplexed look she added, "Don't you know they speculate about all the men, which ones would make good boyfriends and husbands, which ones are handsome but dangerous and only after one thing. It's all they talk about really."

"And you?"

"Oh, I listen but I want more out of life than a husband and kids and nappies on the line. If I'd wanted that I might as well have stayed at home and married one of the local lads. But when the company started visiting the schools to recruit girls I jumped at the chance. Came straight here from school, freezing at the bus stop on a morning and wondering what the hell I'd done. Still, I think it's been worth it."

Bob was fascinated by her, her lust for something better and willingness to be different. He was also very physically attracted to her, more than he had been to any girl for a while. He looked at his watch and was surprised how much time had passed. Grabbing their coats, they ran back to the station and were just in time to jump on the bus. Out of breath and laughing, they took seats together.

"We'll be late back. What will you say to your mother?" He was probing, wondering what her home life was like and, more pertinently, whether she had a boyfriend waiting for her.

"Oh, it will be all right, we never eat dinner until Dad comes in on this shift. So I often do a bit of shopping on my way home or have a coffee with one of the girls. It's why I missed the first bus tonight, I had some things to collect for Mum. So it's her fault." *She giggled again,* he thought. "When I was at school, she would have tea and a cake ready for me to keep me going while I was doing my homework."

"Same here. My mum was old colliery school, the men went to work and the women looked after them and the house. You don't want that, do you? Is there a boy waiting for you to do that for him?"

"That's very personal, Mr Lee." Joan used the title not in deference but more as a pert tease. "And no, there isn't a boy waiting for me to do that and won't be. I'm not going to be anybody's skivvy. What about you, do you have some little woman waiting to look after you. The girls at work are all desperate to find out. I've told them that I know of no one in the village but you'd been away so there may be someone elsewhere."

"Well, there isn't any mysterious long-distance lover and none of the village girls would be interested."

"You'd be surprised. I don't think the men like you very much but a lot of the girls do. I think that some of them find you unusual and something of a challenge," she laughed, "and because they can't understand why any man doesn't find them gorgeous."

"You're more cynical than I am. A rare trait in one so young."

"I try hard old man. We're here by the way, would you like me to help you off the bus?"

"Cheek, would you liked me to see you home to fend off all those young men who find you gorgeous."

"Who says I want them fending off. And you'll only get us talked about. This is a small village remember and I have my reputation to think of. I'll be okay, and I'll see you tomorrow."

"Will you," he was surprised.

"At work silly." She walked down the high street before turning into the warren of streets. He watched her retreating back lost in thought, most of all thinking how much he liked watching her.

Chapter Thirty-Five

Bob did see Joan at work the following day. He found excuses that day, and over the following days, to visit the section where she was. He didn't talk to her, rather nodded, and smiled when no one was looking. More importantly, he made efforts to leave work at the same time so they could travel home together. It wasn't always possible but often enough for a pattern to emerge. They were the best time of the day for him, ones he looked forward to, when he could let his guard down and he was no longer Mr Lee but merely Robbie and Joan. He did begin to think on those journeys as a pair, if not necessarily as a couple.

He enjoyed her company and conversation. She was pert and funny as opposed to his serious and dour, spontaneous to his calculating. Most of all, he enjoyed how she made fun of him, jumping on his comments and making him relax. It took away the worries of the day and became the highlight of the evening.

Things began to change when one of his other plans came to fruition. His life had never been in the village but in the city since he'd started work. He'd thought of living there but for a single man, this was difficult. For some time, he'd been saving and with promotions these had increased. He'd learned to drive during his time in the army and now took the step of buying his first car. It meant going to the city would be easier and into the environment where he was more comfortable. The downside was that he would miss his time with Joan and the thought, to his surprise, was painful. He told her on the journey home that night.

"Well, I won't be doing this much more."

"Doing what?" she asked surprised.

"Getting the bus with you." She looked hurt and turned her head away. When she looked back, she asked if it was something she'd done. He realised his lack of tact and added quickly, "No, I'm buying a car that's all."

"So I'll be on my own then?" she said, biting her lip. She looked so forlorn he could have kicked himself. He also realised that he would miss her. So he quickly explained that they could still travel together and that it would be so much more convenient and easier. He was flustered and stumbling over his words, surprised by her feelings and confused by his own. Looking at his face and confusion, she laughed.

"Well, won't that get you talked about at work. The girls will have a field day. The village will also begin to gossip."

"It's got nothing to do with work. Besides, we live and work in the same place so what is more natural than we travel together. Besides the village can bugger off. Anyway," he added, "I'd miss you." That had come rushing out, surprising both of them, and she put her hand on his automatically before quickly withdrawing it. To hide the embarrassment, she asked what car it was and when was he getting it.

"It's a mini, and I'm picking it up this weekend, so I'll pick you up from Monday, if that's all right. It means you can have a bit of sleep in from now on."

"Extra sleep and a personal chauffeur, what more can a girl want?" She laughed again but he felt an undercurrent. But he was relieved that she'd accepted because he couldn't bear the thought that he wouldn't have time with her again. Bob had never had close friends who he could confide in, and she filled that hole inside him. She could make fun of his idiosyncrasies whilst making him laugh at himself. He was also physically attracted to her but made no move. At first, it was because romantic involvement did not fit in with his plans but now it was because he didn't want to spoil what he had.

"That's it then, 8 o'clock sharp on Monday morning." She looked at him amused.

"Okay, boss. Do you want me to walk to the bus stop? I can wear a pink carnation if you want?" He never knew when she was joking with him or hiding something else.

"Don't be silly, stay warm and dry, I'll come around the house for you. That's unless you're ashamed to be seen with me or you don't want your reputation tarnished?" Now, it was her turn to look abashed.

"I'm never ashamed to be seen with you and to quote you, I don't give a bugger what they think in the village." He was now surprised and the rest of the journey continued in companionable silence.

True to his word, Bob pulled up outside Joan's house at eight sharp, waiting on the road at the end of the garden. Joan's father was a colliery deputy and as an official was entitled to a slightly larger house with an accompanying garden; one of the few in the village though still near all the others. As he sat, he saw several net curtains twitching at neighbours' windows. That was inevitable. As he debated going to the front door, Joan emerged from it; obviously she had been watching for him. He was relieved, he had no desire to meet her parents and going to the front door had other connotations in the village, heralding courtship.

"I'm here," she said unnecessarily, as she got in the car. "Nice, I like this."

"The car or the lift?"

"Both. It's a nice car and very modern and trendy. And yes, I like being chauffeured. Drive on, Robert." She giggled. The joke continued with the only change being that when she got in on a night she changed the instruction to home James and don't spare the horses.

Things continued happily for several weeks. There's was the inevitable gossip at work but they both stuck to their story that they both lived in the same village and it was only logical that they travelled together.

Joan embellished it by challenging the girls, "Look what would you prefer, a nice warm lift door to door or battling through on the bus every day?"

After a while, like all gossip, it stopped for lack of interest. But interest would soon grow again. It happened that both Bob and Joan were working late: it was stocktaking and all the staff were lending a hand. It was no great inconvenience to them as with the car their travel arrangements were flexible.

It was actually early evening when they got away. Comfortably in the car, Bob asked if her tea would be burnt.

"No. Mum won't be in anyway. She'll be at Aunty Betty's as she hasn't been well and Dads on shift. I told her not to worry, I'd call at the fish shop. How about you?"

He laughed, "Believe it or not, I said the same thing. That will be two fish suppers then." As they were talking, they were nearing a country pub that was popular as drink driving laws were still fairly relaxed. It still had a roadhouse feel about it as there was still not many cars about and it, therefore, catered for a fairly well-off clientele. "I tell you what, we can do better than two fish suppers, why don't we stop here for a bite to eat. My treat, I understand it has a pretty good reputation." It had, but Bob had also checked it out when he was trying his new car out.

"Okay, but this will get us talked about if were seen."

"I don't care if you don't." He pulled off the road and parked directly outside the front. "After you, madam." They walked together into a comfortable lounge in the fashion of the day; dark wood, beams, highly polished brasses and thick patterned carpet. "Would you like a drink?"

"That would be nice. A sherry please."

"Not a Babycham girl then?"

"No, it's horrible stuff. My dad calls it overpriced cider for the foolish who think it's posh." She laughed, "He can't stand pretension."

Wise man, thought Bob. He hadn't met her father but from what Joan had said about him, he found himself warming to the man. They found a table near the window as it was still light and it presented a view over the fields to the hills beyond. Bob brought drinks back from the bar together with two menus in leather cases. The waitress had said she'd be over later to take their orders.

Joan opened the menu, "This is nice, what do you fancy?"

The menu was fairly traditional with emphasis on meat and pastry. After several minutes of perusing the options, he laid his menu down, "I think I'll go save and have the scampi, what about you? Pick what you want, I said this is my treat."

"I think I'll join you with the scampi. So it is two fish suppers," she laughed, "or two posh fish suppers, what would my dad say?" When the waitress had taken their orders, Bob asked what she'd told her father about him. "Only that you're a nice man whose giving me a lift to work, oh and that we're getting married on Friday." Bob almost choked on his beer. Seeing his face, she added, "I'm only teasing, silly. I know it's not like that with us."

"It could be if you want." The words came out before he had time to think. "Sorry, I know you wouldn't want that. Don't let it spoil the evening, you're the only person I feel comfortable with." It was her turn to be surprised and as she looked at him her eyes softened.

"It could be if you want it too," she put her hand on his, "can I ask you one question, Mr Lee, what took you so long?"

"Well, you can't rush good things, and of course, I had to wait for the police checks and the medical reports."

"And what did they say?" she asked.

"That you were of good character but that if you went out with me it would prove your insanity." Pulling a mad looking face, she leered at him.

"Guilty as charged." They both laughed. If you'd later asked how the night was, they would both say wonderful, if you'd asked what the food like was, neither could remember. It was a new beginning for them both.

Chapter Thirty-Six

It wasn't the following Friday but a year from the following Saturday that Bob stood outside the village church at the bottom of the long winding terrace that led to the shops and the myriad of social clubs. Meant to be imposing, it was slightly elevated from the rest of the street, its brick structure masked by stone cladding that looked neither ancient nor modern. Unfortunately, the cladding did not extend to the interior which was red brick that, like everything else in the village, suffered from decades of soot. Bob always thought it resembled a public urinal more than a church; an imposing urinal but a urinal never the less. But it was the village church and he was marrying a village girl, something he thought would never happen. But Joan was different and that was what had attracted him in the first place.

Things had moved quickly from that first meal and the kiss goodnight that had followed. For a few weeks, they had kept their growing relationship secret but Joan was unhappy about that. In the end, it was work that had prompted them to emerge as a couple: Bob, as a manager, was obliged by company policy to tell his superior that he was in a relationship with one of the female employees. His boss had simply congratulated him and winked that he had made a good choice with one of the prettiest girls in the office. Bob wasn't sure he liked the insinuation but had merely smiled and let it pass.

Joan had been more open and had simply announced during lunch with her friends at work, "Well, girls, you can stop wondering, Robbie and me are going out. So now it's official."

The girls had gathered around her bombarding her with questions including the inevitable: 'so, its Robbie, now is it'. "It is to me, it's still Mr Lee when you're at work."

Bob and Joan didn't actually work together but exchanged many a discrete smile when they passed. However, they could often be observed holding hands as they left the office and walked to the car.

Bob's world had certainly been turned around and never more so than in the village; Joan had confided in her mother and insisted Bob tell his parents, "It's a small village and she'd be hurt if she found out by local gossip." Although he'd always been reluctant to let other people know his business and been very protective of his personal life, he'd had to agree with her and had broken the news to his mother. She had been delighted, wringing her hands as she tried to contain her excitement telling him a tumble of words that she was so glad, and what a nice girl Joan had always been and what a lovely family they were. She gushed as she asked if he was happy and added just wait till you father hears.

As Bob anticipated, he didn't share his mother's enthusiasm saying bluntly. "It was about bloody time," and adding sarcastically, "she's not short sighted, is she?" Finally, adding, "So you'll be moving out, will you?"

At this, his mother lost her general reserve and snapped, "He's only just met the lass and he can stay here as long as he wants." His normally belligerent father knew better than to argue on the rare occasions she put her foot down. He held his tongue instead.

Now, it was official the things for Bob did change. His life no longer revolved around work and college but the time he spent with Joan which became all consuming. As well as travelling together every morning and evening, it seemed that they couldn't spend enough time together. Many an evening saw them hunting for small county pubs where they could eat; neither were drinkers and there was nowhere in the village that they could retreat to and talk. And talk they did, for hours, taking delight in the fact that they were both dreamers;

Bob, surprised that the seemingly outgoing Joan wanted more and Joan that the apparently practical and dour Bob lived for escape and that everything he did or had done was working towards that. But more importantly was that underlying the romance was the fact that they were friends. Bob, although comfortable with people, had never really formed any close friendships, sharing nothing in common with the people around him and reluctant to share his thoughts for fear of ridicule. But now, he had someone to share with and the words poured out of him. He also listened as Joan opened her heart. She resented the attitudes around her and was strong willed, but underneath, she was fragile.

On the days they didn't drive out, there was little to do apart from the local cinemas of which the village boasted several. Bob cared little for most of the war films that were popular at the time but admired the new wave hitting the screen such as 'Room at the Top', 'A kind of loving' and 'Saturday Night and Sunday Morning'. The films resonated with him with their theme of rebellion and breaking away, of moving up in a world hostile to change.

Joan enjoyed them as well but was more drawn to the romantic element of the films and how the females were stereotyped and seemed to get a raw deal. In Room at the Top, she cried over Alice and despaired over Brenda in Saturday Night. She was virulently annoyed with Ingrid saying she should grow up and stand up to her mother. Bob was amused, but also welcomed her different perspective of the films. He couldn't think of anyone else he could watch or talk about them with.

As time wore on and they were increasingly together, it was inevitable that they should decide to get married. Neither of them made the decision alone and in many ways, it was similar to how their courtship began. As they sat in the lounge of a small pub next to the cinema enjoying a quiet drink before he walked her home, reluctant to end the evening, and holding hands she said, "I hate this time of day, when we have to say goodnight. I'd rather go home with you."

"So would I but it's no good just wishing. We need to do something about it." To her look of incredulity and hope he added, "Do you think we should get married?" Seeing the look on her face, he said, "You know I love you." To her 'you've never told me before', he said, "I always have, from the first moment I saw you. But I didn't want to scare you away."

"You silly, you would never scare me away and I love you too. It's about time we get that out of the way. Of course, I'll marry you, with all my heart. But what are we going to do? I don't want to live here and you have never had any intention of staying here." To his 'I would for you', she interjected, "Thanks but it would drive you mad."

He laughed, "Madder, you mean."

She smiled, "You've never been mad, insufferable sometimes but never mad. I could never love a madman. But we need to decide what we are going to do."

They talked throughout the rest of the evening, the conversation going backwards and forwards until Bob's head spun; talking about ceremonies, receptions, families and to Bob more importantly, where they were going to live. He would happy if the two of them had gone away and married quietly, if not just lived together but that would be for a later time. In the end they agreed it would be best if they moved to the city, it was near work and a better environment for them.

At Bob's insistence, they agreed that they would save and buy a house; it would probably be small but would, as Bob said, get them on the property ladder. In the end, after extra drinks that they weren't used to, they left and wound their way back to Joan's house. At the door, he went to kiss her goodnight, as usual, before he went home.

"Oh, no, you don't, you can come in. In fact, you'd better come in," they went in through the front door and Bob thought, *to hell let the neighbours talk.* From the small vestibule at the bottom of the stair, they turned into the front room where Joan's mother sat with her father. Bob liked the fact that they used the front room instead of living at the back of the house like the rest of the village.

It could be, he thought, *because they had a garden and the door didn't lead off the street.* But if was nice to see them sitting together although he felt his apprchension growing. Joan's mother looked up surprised as they walked in although she welcomed him with a 'hello Robbie'.

Joan didn't wait for any questions but launched in with a fast, "You've met Robbie, Dad, well we've got some news for you, Robbie has asked me to marry him and I've said yes." Her mother jumped up and embraced her daughter as they both laughed and cried and gabbled a hundred questions. Her father looked at Bob.

"I don't remember you asking me for permission." As he saw the look of horror on Bob's face, he too laughed. "I'm only winding you up, son. I'm glad for the pair of you. But you could have given me more warning. I need a drink. There's a bottle of whisky, you'll join me." It wasn't a question and Bob accepted the proffered glass as gratefully as he could. "I'm glad it's you, did you know she never stops talking about you, its Robbie this and Robbie that. Now we can answer her back as we get to know you better. Don't be a stranger here, we won't bite. What do your parents think?"

"We haven't told them yet. We thought you should be the first to know." When he saw the look of scepticism on his face, he came clean. "That's not totally true, we only decided tonight and when we got here, Joan said I had to come in."

"Clever lad. If there's one thing I've learnt, it's that when a woman makes up her mind, a wise man does as he's told. So you've passed that test. Have you thought where you're going to live? Joan won't want to live around here, I can tell you that. She's no snob, but this village isn't for her."

"Yes, we've talked about it. We think the city, it's where we both work and near enough so she can see you two. We'd like to buy a house but will have to start small. I've got some savings towards a deposit but we'll have to save for a while but we'll get there. You don't mind if we wait a little for the ceremony?"

"Of course I don't mind, it will give me time to save up as well. Our Joan will only want the best." Joan turned around at that point.

"That's right, and you're going to pay." Both Joan and her father laughed. *That's how it should be,* thought Bob, so different from his own father. He decided he liked Joan's father and the more he met him, the more his liking grew. Unlike his own father, he knew he'd had no choice in the occupation he followed, but respected anyone who tried to better themselves and welcomed Bob into the family.

As they were saving hard, Bob spent ever-increasing time at Joan's where her mother spoilt him outrageously. Although an only child, Joan seemed to have a myriad of cousins who he came to know; the female ones being most curious about meeting 'our Joan's fella'. But her male cousins also called and in a bizarre kind of a way, Bob found himself becoming part of the village just as he was about to leave. His acceptance also spread to his father. His workmates congratulated him that his son was marrying George's daughter 'who was a grand lass and he seemed a canny lad'.

If affection, didn't increase, he now earned a little more respect from him. Bob's mother absolutely revelled in the attention she got from her friends. Although Bob generally spent most of their time at Joan's; using the excuse that if she came to his home, he would only have to walk her home and then walk back, Joan insisted on visiting his mother, calling for Sunday lunch and even making him go to the club for a pint with his father before they sat down to eat.

Yes, it's been a funny kind of year, thought Bob as he stood outside the church with his best man; one of his college friends. Neil, his friend, was a city boy and found the village amusing. The night before, he had stayed with Bob and they had followed tradition and called for a drink with his father and then Joan's. Bob had no desire for a drunken bachelor night, much to the disappointment of Joan's cousins who had more or less adopted him and joined them later in the evening insisting that it was bad luck if he didn't have a drink with them.

Bob had complied, but had managed to drink less than the others whose revelry enlivened the bar. Joan, on the other hand, had celebrated her hen night two days earlier in the city with the girls from work in one of the Italian restaurants that were starting to become popular. On reflection, Bob thought he'd rather have been there himself but he had no intention of rocking the boat now that they would bc lcaving. They'd sank every penny they had into buying a small Victorian artisans' cottage in the city. It needed work but they were young and keen and had done enough so far to allow them move in. It was a start and near to the centre and work and had put them on the property ladder.

To his surprise, his father had been supportive of his decision seeing it less as social climbing and more becoming less dependent on the tied houses that went with work in the village and, as he put it, 'made you less at the beck and call of the bosses'.

Even more to his surprise, his father had said to him a few days before the wedding, "Look, son, George is paying for the wedding which is his right as father of the bride. But I'll never have to do that so your mother and I want to help. You're not having a honeymoon so why don't you take the girl somewhere nice on the night." With that he'd given him an envelope telling him to open it later. When he did, he found it held four neatly folded five-pound notes. Joan had cried when he told her.

As he stood lost in thought, Neil nudged him on the arm, "Time to go in, mate."

Yes, it's time, he thought as they entered the cold church. It was a warm day outside but it never seemed to reach the interior which was always gloomy. But today, he wasn't gloomy, today was the start of the rest of his life and he was eager for it to begin. He was so eager to move on that the day developed a serene and dreamlike quality. He was aware, having been woken by the wedding march, of Joan walking in on the arm of her father, looking beautiful in her wedding dress.

He vaguely remembered standing outside for photographs and going into the welfare hall which had been hired for the reception. The dull speeches that followed with the obligatory reading of the cards; he'd warned Neil not to be too flamboyant with his speech, and the thanks to the bridesmaids who were more cousins. Neil took delight in this as the girls took an interest in him.

The traditional tongue and ham lunch followed and the toasts before they found themselves saying goodbye to the guests and thanking them for coming. After Joan had changed into her going away outfit, they went outside where Bob had earlier parked his car. The cousins had taken delight in attaching tin cans to it but Bob thought 'so what', he'd get rid of them later. As they drove away and left the village, he thought, *Goodbye.*

In the city, Bob had used his father's money to book them into a hotel for the night. Strangely, it was the same hotel where Fred and Ivy had celebrated their wedding years before. Post austerity, it had been re-decorated and refurbished, but retained its pre-war elegance.

"This is nice," Joan commented as they registered at reception as Mr and Mrs Lee.

"This is the start of a new life for us." She smiled as he led her to their room.

Chapter Thirty-Seven

Whilst Bob and Joan were moving to the city, Duncan and Ruby were planning to leave. Or rather, Ruby was planning. After Fred and Ivy's wedding, they had married quietly and eventually moved from her small house to a tied property belonging to the university. This was in an imposing terrace next to the college that would ultimately become separated when a new access road to the city was built between the two. Planning for this development; which would decimate parts of the old centre, had already been approved and was one of the reasons for her desire to leave.

However, the main reason was to get Duncan away. Ruby was aware, and indeed had always been aware, of Duncan's activities and affairs. She had learned to tolerate them during their strange relationship. In many ways, Duncan reminded her of her father whom she'd adored. Bur he was also the child she would never have and she treated his affairs like an indulgent mother knowing that he would always come running back to Mummy. Besides, she knew that the women he slept with actually meant nothing to him. But university life was narrow, the city was small, and as Duncan cut swathes through wives and students tongues wagged, and if there was one thing Ruby couldn't abide, it was to be the butt of jokes and snide remarks.

The impetus to move came, strangely, from Alex. Duncan returned one Friday night from his usual drink with the boys and mentioned that Alex had told him they were planning a big development for the village on the outskirts of the city where both he and Fred lived. It was intended, he said, to use the old village as the basis of a new suburb for the city and that, initially, they were selling plots for houses. Anyone buying now could build to their own design and that anyone who had any sense should get in quick whilst land prices were cheap.

At first, Duncan was not keen on the idea, happy as he said to live rent free and near to work. Ruby was ready for his arguments and pointed out that Duncan had just received money from his fathers will which he needed investing and that bricks and mortar was a safe option. In addition, they would still be living rent-free. Her career was also going well and would easily cover any additional costs. The final, and crucial argument, was that he would be near Alex and Fred. As Duncan wavered, she produced the glossy advertising she had got from the developers extolling the benefits of the new lifestyle including garaging and parking. When she said it would be worth getting a new car, she knew she'd won.

For Ruby, there was also another reason for the move: she missed Ivy more than she cared to admit. At work, she was surrounded by people but she was a senior manager and kept her distance, developing a reputation for being efficient but something of a cold fish. Since Ivy had left following Christopher's birth, she had no one to confide in. She missed the time they had lived together when Ivy was the closest thing to the sister she never had, someone she could trust and who understood her, if not fully, then closer than anyone else had. It was with delight that, with her usual efficiency, she set about planning the house, meeting with solicitors, architects, planners and builders.

She didn't want just any house, she wanted a statement, like at work, she wanted to be the best to prove that the girl who had fought her way out of gentile poverty was a success and that no one would know where she had come from or who she was. Duncan, on the other hand, didn't care one iota about the house being content with himself. But as long as Ruby was dealing with all the details, he was content to take a back seat as she bustled and bullied her way through the build. She chose a plot near the high street at the edge of the new development opposite the church and the Victorian pub. More importantly, it was opposite the house Fred and Ivy had moved into after their marriage.

The build had progressed smoothly as the large three bedroomed detached house rose from the foundations: the architect had argued that the size of the property could easily accommodate five bedrooms but Ruby was adamant that she wanted three decent sized rooms and that new innovation of an en-suite. It was a house for her and Duncan to live in, not for raising a family or accommodating guests. This included a downstairs study for Duncan, plenty of parking and a high wall that gave it seclusion: there might have been plans for a substantial estate behind the house but that didn't mean that Ruby would be part of it. She wanted the modernity of it, together with all the conveniences it brought, but had no interest in the 'hoi polloi' as she called them. It wasn't that she was necessarily a snob, she genuinely had no interest in other people and no desire to mix with them.

If Ruby had no desire to mix, she'd forgotten about Duncan's gregariousness. He needed company, or more honestly, an audience to charm. The house became the centre of the social scene in the village. At first, this had been confined to Ivy and Fred and the ever-present Alex. Ruby was content with this; she still found Fred difficult but was delighted to see Ivy and Alex was always the steady one and the peacemaker of the group. But Duncan needed a wider audience to impress and started inviting new neighbours as the estate developed. The grounds were large enough to accommodate a party, secluded behind the high walls and it became a highlight for anyone on the estate to be invited. Ruby was not surprised that the men invited all had pretty wives but consoled herself that at least here she could keep an eye on him. Ivy also discretely monitored his activities.

Ruby and Ivy's relationship was changing. In the beginning, she had been Ivy's boss and protector, then when they'd lived together, her big, if bossy, sister. Bur since her marriage, and certainly since Christopher had been born, things had changed. Now, it was Ivy who had grown and become more dominant. She was the only person who could correct Ruby or, more importantly, the only person Ruby would allow to. She understood Ruby more than anyone else, had witnessed the starchy section officer in the army, seen through the frostiness to the vulnerability underneath as their friendship grew and how she used her cold front to control people at work.

But on an evening, she saw the other side as they talked through the events of the day and the front dropped. She had even on one occasion asked about her childhood and had seen, despite her reticence, the pain in her eyes. She also knew how she loved Duncan, not the Duncan now but the Duncan that she'd got to know in the army, the Duncan who opened up to her and shared his feelings.

Duncan still talked to Ruby but now the conversations were about practical and superficial things. Duncan was, indeed, a superficial creature now. The shield he had raised was now an integral part of him. Only injury and disability had ever pierced that emotional reserve and only Ruby had witnessed it.

Chapter Thirty-Eight

Bob and Joan were the happy young newlyweds when they moved into their first home together. It was small and terraced, a proper city house that opened of the street with no garden. But it was in a quiet street and near the centre and therefore, work. It needed work and modernisation but that had been reflected in the price. Most importantly, it was theirs and they were together, on an adventure when the world was changing. When either of them looked back, they would have agreed it was the happiest time of their lives. Youth, freedom and each other.

They set to in renovating and modernising the house as money and time allowed, spare time was overtaken with scraping walls and decorating after builders had made structural changes or necessary repairs. They didn't care, laughing as they worked before dashing to one of the numerous Italian restaurants that were springing up across the city or branching out into a cheap Chinese before running back to fall into bed together. It was the start of the sixties and they were going to be the hip young couple.

In time, the house took shape, fashionable for the time, with a great deal of Hygena and flat pack furniture. Nothing was going to be traditional with both of them determined to move as far away from the past they had grown up with. With friends and an active social scene, life was good and for several years they enjoyed themselves. But as with all generation's things began to change as their friends were first getting married and then starting families.

To both their surprise, Joan began to long for a baby as she visited friends who had given birth and the girls at work began to leave one by one. At this point in his life, Bob wasn't in the least paternal but loved Joan and went along with her wishes. They'd been married for several years with no hint of pregnancy and were amazed how quickly Joan found herself with child once the decision had been made. Days were now spent planning for the new arrival and as Joan blossomed he found he loved her more, reassuring her as the pounds added to her waistline that it didn't change anything.

Two things did change however. As Bob saw his new born son for the first time, something happened inside him and feelings emerged that he didn't think he possessed. He vowed to himself, at that point, that no son of his would go through the experiences he'd had. The second was when they brought young Neil home. Their bijou house, that had suited them both so well, suddenly seemed cramped as they tried to fit in prams and all the other paraphernalia that accompanied a baby.

There was also no garden to put the pram or for the child to play in. Bob had continued to do well and had just been promoted to assistant branch manager ahead of a lot of the older men. His salary increase more than compensated for the loss of Joan's. A lot of people in the city were now moving out to the new satellite suburbs that were springing up away from the grime and bustle of the city. Houses that had garages drives and gardens. Homes with all mod cons including central heating and bathrooms and separate cloakrooms. It was a move up the housing chain, something always close to Bob's heart. Bob still had a need to show the world that he was a success. Joan was less keen on the idea; she could still see her friends at work for a coffee whilst they lived in the city but was convinced by the thought of the open space and that it was a better place to bring up Neil.

Her only question to Bob was: "Do you think we can afford it?"

"Of course, we can. It might be a bit tight at first but it will be worth it in the end. You know me, I would never get us into a situation we couldn't afford." Joan couldn't argue with that and so it was dccidcd that thcy would start looking around. As it happened, the estate they chose was in the village where Fred and Ivy had settled next to Alex and where

Duncan and Ruby had commissioned their home. They couldn't afford to commission as Duncan and Ruby had, but looked at some of the properties released by the builder.

Strangely, these were near the edge of the estate near where the purpose-built houses were. For all her reticence about the move, Joan was captivated by the house they viewed. Detached, with three bedrooms and an additional downstairs cloakroom it was a far cry from the terraced colliery houses they'd grown up in. Large windows let in light and increased the feeling of space and gardens to both the front and rear were an added attraction. Even more, she liked the feel of the village with its Victorian church and high street and stone-built pub. They'd parked the car and gone with the pram for a walk around after viewing the house.

"Well, what do you think?" asked Bob

"It's perfect, Robbie. It's so clean and open here and the house is more than I ever dreamed of. There's even a school for Neil in a few years. But are you sure we can afford it?"

"I've told you we can. It's our time now. Do we go for it? I want the best for us and young Neil."

"Yes, yes, yes." Joan was excited, laughing and crying at the same time. Bob put his arm around, glancing at Neil in his pram. Yes, everything was perfect. Within days, the 'for sale' sign went up outside their house as the 'sold' sigh was erected outside their new home. Bob dealt with solicitors, estate agents and building societies as Joan planned the decorating and furniture that was needed. In excitement, they drove on a night to the estate and sat outside looking at the place planning and dreaming.

At last, the day of the move arrived. Their old house had sold very quickly and, on the day of completion, Bob collected the keys from the agent and, once the removals had loaded their furniture, handed over the keys to their old home. Joan had sat in the car as he did this; in those days you could still park on the street, before they set off to their new place.

"Any regrets?" he asked.

"A few. We've been happy here."

"And we'll be happy where we're going. We both agreed that the move was going to be the best for all of us." She smiled and they drove to unload their furniture.

The van was outside when they arrived and they set to moving in. Neil was at Grandma's for the day. Bob would fetch him later when the work was done and his room was ready. It wasn't like before when they'd had to move what they could as they renovated. It was a new house and decorated by the builder who'd also had the carpets laid. With a minimum of fuss, and the help of the removal men, their furniture was in place. It looked lost in the larger rooms but the basics were there and they would add to them over the coming years.

Bob left to pick up Neil and Joan's mother who wanted to help Joan unpack and clean. He listened to her chatter in the car and answered her questions as she fussed over Neil who cooed with all the attention. She expressed her admiration as they pulled into the village and stopped outside the house.

The only adverse comment she made was: "By, you've got some nosy neighbours," she said as she saw Duncan, who under the pretence of washing the car, was watching the move and Joan moving around.

"He's only washing his car," said Bob irritated. He didn't see Ruby who was at an upstairs window, watching Duncan as he watched Joan.

Chapter Thirty-Nine

At first, it seemed Bob was right about the move. It was still warm and the house needed little attention being new. It was nice not having to spend time decorating and planning the next improvement and having extra time to spend with Neil. She spent the last of the fine weather exploring the village, pushing Neil in his pram and calling in at the local shops. But the village was small and the number of shops limited. After a while, she found herself missing the excitement of sitting with Bob planning the next thing they were going to do or working together and then dashing for a drink.

Bob was busy at work coping with the demands of his promotion and was content to sit on a night tired after the day's events. Joan also missed the girls at work and the gossip and silliness of office life. To put it mildly, she was bored and the boredom was starting to lead to depression. When Bob's boss had asked how she was coping, he'd said fine.

But his Boss had sensed something was wrong and in a backhanded kind of way had offered comfort, "Never mind, lad, it's normal, they all get a little down after they have the first child. My wife was the same."

Bob wasn't comforted, but kept his own council. He tried on an evening to tell her what had gone on at work but the detail didn't interest her, it was the girls she missed and his conversation only emphasised what she was missing. In the end, he stopped talking and the distance between them began to grow until, in the end, there was only silence and the television.

Joan strangely missed the village. She may have been an only child, but she had a myriad of cousins and when she went out, she was always guaranteed to bump into someone she knew. Now she felt she was among strangers and didn't belong. She'd been among strangers in the city but she'd had another life and that wasn't important; she was master of her own destiny and her own person. But that confidence had now gone and there was an emptiness where it had been.

She was Bob's wife and Neil's mother but where was Joan? She went about the upkeep of the house with her usual efficiency but not enthusiasm. It was spotless, Bob's shirts were immaculate and dinner was always ready. She wondered what had happened to the girl who was going to be no man's skivvy and concluded she had merely exchanged one trap for another. Not that Bob expected anything and he was still the kind man she'd fallen in love with. But at least she still had Neil and she doted on him, talked to him when he was too young to understand what she said and fussed him needlessly when her need, not his, demanded it.

Autumn continued that way into winter when one day she found the walls closing in on her and needed to get out for the day. Although it was early December, it was a fine day and she decided to head into the city to do some Christmas shopping. She could have gone with Bob, but he was busy at work and she wanted to go now. Dressing the growing Neil, she put him in his pushchair and took the bus into the city. He was at the age when he was paying attention and delighted with the ride and the displays in the shops. She didn't want very much but it was an excuse to be out and enjoy the comfort of the crowd and the festive air.

Neil also offered some company and she felt less alone and more her old self, treating herself to a coffee as she fed Neil his lunch. As twilight descended early, they gloried in the lights coming on across the old market square and the lights glowing on the tree there. The weather had started to turn and she decided she had to get home. It would have been sensible to call at the store and get a lift home with Bob, but she knew he would be working late during the busiest time of the year for the company.

The old bus station would be busy and she decided to walk to a stop on the outskirts of the city to catch the local service. It had grown colder as the pale sun dipped below the horizon and she had started to regret her decision not to catch Bob at work when a large car pulled up at the stand and she heard her name being called.

She didn't know the car but when the door opened, she recognised the driver as one of her neighbours; a tall middle-aged handsome man who had the large house on the corner. "It is Joan, isn't it, don't stand there in the cold, I'm heading home so let me give you a lift."

She was cold, the idea of a lift was attractive and he wasn't exactly a stranger. She thanked him and he helped her into the car with Neil and put his pushchair in the large boot.

As they drove away he said, "That's better, isn't it? By the way we haven't been introduced, my name is Duncan."

"Nice to meet you, especially on such a cold day and its good of you to give us a lift."

"It's not a problem. I'm heading home anyway so it's hardly an inconvenience. Where's your husband today?"

"Bob's still at work, it's their busiest time of the year. How are you home so early?"

"I'm at the university and all the students are heading home for Christmas. I could do things there but I thought if I don't need to be there I might as well come home and work in the warm rather than in my drafty rooms. Besides, if I had, I wouldn't have had the chance to pick up my pretty neighbour. I've been meaning to have a word with you and it seems an ideal time to do it."

"Oh, and why is that?" He laughed at her obvious embarrassment.

"Sorry, that wasn't very well put. What must you think of me? What I meant was it was opportune to meet you because I've been meaning to have a chat with you and your husband for a while. We are having a party just before Christmas for a few friends and neighbours and wondered if you and your husband would like to come and meet people. We're not a bad crowd. It's nothing fancy, just a few pre-prandial drinks in the early evening. Please say you'll come."

"We'd love too, but as you can see we have young Neil here."

"That's not a problem, bring him with you. It's early and you can go whenever you like. Ivy usually brings young Christopher with her. Although he's growing up rapidly and it won't be long before the girls will be looking at him. Handsome little devil, takes after his mother." He laughed, "Fred's a lovely man but hardly dashing."

"Okay, I'll talk to Bob. I'd love to come and it's nice of you to invite us. To be honest, it will be nice to get out and have some fun. It's been quiet since we came here and I'd like to meet some new people. Your wife must have felt the same when she had babies?"

"Not really. We haven't any children. Ruby's a career woman. Enough of that, I look forward to seeing you there. Speaking of which, here we are." Duncan pulled the car up outside her house, got the pushchair out of the boot and carried it to the door.

"Thanks very much, you're a real gentleman." Duncan smiled as, with Neil in her arms, she let herself in through the front door. He put the chair in the hall and with, "I'll see you at the party then," left turning to give a last grin. "That was a nice man," she said to Neil who merely gurgled in reply. Joan felt happier than she had for a while and looked forward to telling Bob the news.

Bob arrived home at half past six to find a buoyant Joan in the kitchen happily cooking dinner. It brightened his day to see her so content; he wasn't oblivious to her depression of late and had felt at a loss over what to do about it. "It looks like someone's has had a good day. What have you been up to?"

"I've been down the city shopping with Neil. He loved all the shops with their lights and music. You should have seen his face."

"Good, I wonder if he would still feel the same if he'd been in the middle of it all day getting trampled by desperate shoppers. But I'm pleased you enjoyed yourselves. But why didn't you come to the store and come home with me? It's gone decidedly chilly now."

"That's the best bit," she grinned. "I didn't come to the store because I knew you'd be busy and I didn't want to disturb you. I remember what it was like in the run up to Christmas. Besides, you needed to work late and I wanted to get Neil home to feed him and give him his bath. He was tired, the little man has had a busy day. He's in his playpen but don't disturb him. He was having a nap the last time I checked him. Anyway, we went to the bus stop to get the 86 back when a car pulled up and someone called my name."

"Who was it?"

"That's the funny part. It was Duncan, the guy who lives in the big house on the corner. He gave me and Neil a lift home. You're right, it was getting cold and I was just wishing I'd gone to the store when he turned up."

Bob's curiosity was raised. "What was he like?" he asked.

"Very nice actually, a bit smooth and debonair but a gentleman. He works at the university but got away early because all the students have gone home for Christmas."

"It's all right for some, the rest of us are working flat out because of it. So what else did he say?"

"That was the best part. He said he'd been wanting to meet us and was glad he'd bumped into me. He also said that he and his wife; Ruby that is, were having friends in before Christmas for drinks and we've been invited. He also said it was early so we could take Neil so there's no problem with babysitters."

"What did you say?"

"I said I'd love to but I'd ask you first. Please say yes, we haven't been out for ages?"

"You do realise we won't know anyone there, don't you?"

"That's the whole point. We never will unless we get out. It's okay for you, you're out at work all day while I'm stuck in here. It's lovely here but I get bored." He could sense her mood changing.

"Okay, we'll go if it keeps you happy. I know when I'm beat." She flung her arms around him.

"Thank you. You never know you might even enjoy yourself, Mr Misery Guts. I'll pop a note in tomorrow."

"Won't his wife be in so you can just call?"

"No, apparently she's in the civil service, some bigwig career woman."

"You've found out quite a lot for a car trip."

"I'm good at that. That's how I met my husband."

"Good looking chap is he, your husband?"

"Absolutely." That night, they fell into bed and it was like it used to be.

Chapter Forty

The day of the party arrived and the weather stayed fair. Not that they had far to travel but the little sun breaking through lifted the spirits. Their spirits hardly needed lifting, Joan had been full of excitement all week and had driven Bob mad about what she should wear. His usual tactic 'you look good in everything': that to him was true, failed to work and he was presented with a veritable fashion parade as dresses were tried on and then discarded. He didn't care; he was a happy to see Joan happy. He was also quite content himself, the invite meant that they were being accepted and status and reputation were important to him.

Finally, Joan had decided on a simple box cut crotchet dress that suited her petite figure and was short enough to emphasise her good legs. At Joan's insistence, he had abandoned his usual suits and was dressed in tapered trousers, button collated shirt and Arran cardigan she'd bullied him into buying. Even Neil was dressed for the occasion. In the late afternoon, after Joan had been watching the house to make sure people had arrived before them, they walked up to the house, through the gates in the walled garden and up to the door, Joan carrying young Neil whilst Bob rang the doorbell.

The door was opened by a beaming Duncan. "Great, you made it, you must be Robbie. Good to meet you. I've already meant your charming wife. Come on in out of the cold."

They followed Duncan into the long hallway where he took their coats as Bob admired the house with its high finish that spoke of quality. It was obvious that as Bob's father would have said 'they're not short of a bob or two'.

"Nice house," commented Bob as Duncan took his coat. "Do you have family?"

"No, there's just Ruby and me. I admit it's a bit big for just the two of us but I had a tied house from the university before and I think they were intended for Victorian professors with twelve children and you get used to the space and so when we had this place built we thought why skimp. Besides, we could afford it so we thought why not. Come on through and meet the rest of the gang."

He led them into a lounge which opened onto a dining room through double doors which were now open to enlarge the room and accommodate the guests. He took them to a pretty but austere looking woman who was standing with another woman of a similar age and a young boy just entering his teens.

"This is Ruby, my good lady," he said putting his arm around the austere woman, "and this her oldest friend, Ivy. And this handsome young fellow is Ivy's son Christopher." He ruffled the boy's hair as he said this. "Where's Fred?" he addressed the woman called Ivy.

"Where do you think?" She said indicating with her shoulder to the dining room where a bar had been set up. "He went to get Ruby and me a drink but seems to have got side tracked. Go tell him he's neglecting his duties and to get Joan a drink. What will you have, dear?"

"A sherry would be nice."

"Wise choice. You're too young to join the old girl's gin and tonic brigade." To Duncan, "Take Robbie with you and let us girls have a chat."

"Uncle Duncan," this from Christopher. "Can I put some decent music on? I've brought my records." He nodded to the radiogram which was emitting some gentle swing at a low volume.

"Okay, young man. Play some of your infernal rock and roll. But nothing too raunchy." Turning to the others, "I'm sure he's turning into a Liverpudlian." Christopher scowled and his mother added, "And not too loud. Joan felt sorry for the boy."

"I like the Mersey sound, what have you got?"

"At last someone with taste. It makes a change from these old fogies who still think it's 1946. What would you like?"

"The Searchers if you have it. Or Billy J Kramer." He scowled at that. "Or anything by the Beatles." He smiled and dashed off with an 'anything you want, madam.'

"I think you've an admirer, young lady," laughed Ivy. Joan missed Ruby's mumbled 'and not just one'. However, Ivy noticed and quickly changed the subject. "And who is this handsome young chap," indicating Neil. "Can I have a hold of him?"

"Of course." She handed Neil to Ivy who cradled and tickled him under his chin. Neil gurgled on cue and they chatted happily until they heard a disturbance at the back of the dining room where a woman was confronting Duncan. A look of pure malice contorted Ruby's face.

"I didn't know you'd invited Gerry and Dianne," Ivy asked Ruby.

"I didn't. They came in with the others and I didn't want to cause a scene. Seems I wasted my time." She gestured to a timid looking man who was watching horrified. "Gerry, I think Dianne's had enough, you'd better get her home." Gerry complied and pulled a protesting Dianne from the house. Once they had left, the room settled down very quickly again. "She can't hold her drink, I'll tell Fred not to give her so much next time."

"There won't be a next time," said Ruby through tight lips. Just then the mood was broken as 'Needles and Pins' burst from the radiogram and a triumphant Christopher emerged from the crowd.

"Found it," he announced happily. "Now you have to dance with me."

"Do you mind," she asked Ivy holding Neil.

"Not at all, I'll look after your baby while you look after mine," she laughed although Christopher only scowled. The rest of the afternoon passed merrily and quickly and it was soon time to say goodbye so they could get Neill ready for his bath and bed. Reluctantly, in Joan's case, they left the party and went home.

Chapter Forty-One

That night, as Bob and Joan lay together, after Neil had been fed, bathed and put to bed, they talked over the events of the afternoon.

"Did you have a good time?" he asked as she snuggled against him.

"What, just now or this afternoon?" she had giggled in reply.

"Not now, this afternoon, silly." As he said this, he was content, things had been quiet between them physically lately and he was happy that she was more her old self.

"Actually, I had a good time. It was nice to be out with adults again. I love Neil but its wearing being with him all the time on my own. You're at work all day with people. It's was nice to be there but also to meet some of the neighbours. I always knew everybody back in the village and it didn't matter in the city because I was at work all day. At least now that I know the neighbours, I don't feel so isolated. Mind you, I don't think I'll be seeing much of that Dianne, what was all that about?"

"I'm not sure, I asked Fred, but all he said was it was the drink talking and Alex didn't say anything. Mind you, he doesn't say very much at all. Fred, on the other hand, never shuts up, but he's good company. Likes a drink mind."

"I gathered that. I was with Ivy; his wife. She's nice, it was her son who was dancing with me. It was a bit of a laugh, he's a nice boy but he must get bored with the old company all the time. They are a lot older than us but they are nice, well most although I'm not sure of Ruby. She's a bit severe but polite all the same. Apparently, she's something in the civil service, Ivy told me she was also in the army with her during the war. An officer no less and Ivy's boss. It's also where she and Ivy met Duncan who was something of a war hero. I rather like him, he's quite dashing but I don't know what he sees in Ruby. What did you talk about?" Bob felt a twinge of jealously as she said this.

"Nothing so interesting, Fred was cracking jokes and knocking back the drink. But he was fun for all of that. Apparently, he's the head of one of the schools in the next village and a bit of a tarter with the kids but well respected. Alex dropped that into the conversation. He's very protective of him. He's also the godfather of your young boyfriend. He found it amusing that the lad has a crush on you. He seems to be the shepherd of the flock. It was him who stepped in when Dianne kicked off and helped Gerry get her out. He's something of a peacemaker. The others all defer to him. I did feel sorry for that Gerry, I only spoke to him briefly but he seemed okay. He was mortified when the row erupted. Poor man! Still it was a good afternoon." He paused, "Actually, Fred and Alex have invited me for a drink. Apparently, they go to the local pub every Tuesday and Friday night and have invited me to join them. I wouldn't mind, if you don't?"

"Robbie Lee consorting with the locals in a pub," she laughed, "what is the world coming to. Of course, I don't mind, it will do you good, you can talk about something else other than work, and then you can come home and tell me all the gossip." She snuggled back into him and he was happy.

The following day, Ivy was also snuggled up against Alex in bed. Fred and Christopher were at school whilst Alex, like Duncan, had finished college for the holidays. Ivy, at a loose end, had gone for a coffee and a chat and one thing had led to another. Since that first time they had, despite protestations that it wouldn't happen again, occasionally slept together. It generally occurred when Fred had another of his bad spells and she'd gone for a shoulder to cry on. But this time, she had gone to talk about Duncan and Ruby.

They lay together in his comfortable bedroom; Alex steadfastly refused to change his lounge which had become more of a study but over the years but Ivy had nagged him into modernising his bedroom, bathroom and kitchen. It wasn't that she intended moving in with him, she would never leave Fred, and although she didn't love Alex, she cared for him deeply and looked out for his welfare. She'd known for a long time that he would never remarry, he'd loved once and death had not diminished that. Sex between them was for comfort and companionship.

At last, she spoke, "So what was all that fuss about with Dianne and Gerry? I thought they were all close."

"Let's just say it was Duncan's and Dianne's closeness that caused all the problems. You must have known?"

"Call me dense, I know Duncan well but I didn't think he would mess about so close to home."

"That was the problem. Ruby found out and raised all hell and threatened to throw him out. She's always known Duncan was having flings but whilst they weren't serious or close to home she turned a blind eye. I don't think for one moment she liked it but she put up with it rather than lose Duncan. I think that's what rattled him when she threatened to throw him out. Anyway, he broke it off with Dianne immediately after she gave him the ultimatum. But as you saw, she wasn't happy about being ditched."

"So why did Ruby invite them to the party?"

"That's the whole point, she didn't. But when Dianne found out about it, she turned up with Gerry. Poor bloke doesn't know anything about it and I feel sorry for him. So I mistakenly tried to keep him away from the fray with Fred and me. But Dianne was practically plastered when she arrived and we left her to continue drinking. Obviously, when she'd had enough Dutch courage, she confronted Duncan. That's when I stepped in to get her out before things got seriously out of control. We passed it off that she'd had too much to drink and let Gerry take her home."

"Why didn't Ruby tell me? And what was Duncan thinking about. I thought he and Gerry were friends."

"You know Ruby better than anyone. She may put up with things but she'll never lose face. As for Duncan, you don't know his favourite expression, pardon the language but 'you can always get new friends but a fuck is a fuck'. Sorry about that."

"That's awful. Is he so selfish? Does he really think so little of people?"

"I don't think it's that, Duncan needs to be admired and wanted, especially by women. He wasn't always like that. You wouldn't have recognised the young Duncan I first knew. Anyway, that's all settled but he'd better be careful now, Ruby's patience only goes so far."

"You don't think he'd mess about so close to home again, do you?"

"With Duncan, you never know. With him, it's practically a compulsion. Take your Christopher's new girlfriend." Ivy laughed.

"Joan, she lovely." She paused, "You're not saying he's set his sights on her, do you?"

"Who do you think invited her and Bob to the party. The man has been on about how pretty she is since they moved in. Every time we have a drink, he mentions it. It might help if you keep an eye on her. She seems a nice kid, but that will only add to the attraction for him."

"Fred's never mentioned it when he comes back from the pub."

"I doubt he even noticed it. He's your husband, you know in many ways he's an innocent. It's why the war messed him up."

Chapter Forty-Two

Joan was happy. Since Christmas, and more especially since Duncan's and Ruby's party, her life had improved. They had become a part of Duncan's set and regular attenders at events at his house. She was also beginning to feel more a part of the community; Ivy would often call for a coffee and, as she jokily put it; to keep an eye on her. When Cristopher was free, he would come to and follow her around like a pet. Although amused, she didn't make any jokes to spare his feelings, besides which Neil adored him and now walking, would make straight for him as soon as he entered the house. She felt sorry for him, within his parent's tight circle of friends he was the only child. She asked Ivy about this one afternoon when they were having coffee.

"Yes, it's a shame, dear but I found one child was quite enough and there's no way Duncan and Ruby would have a family, gracious could you imagine Duncan as a father?" They both laughed at the thought. After a moment's pause, she'd added quietly, "Alex would have done but he's content to be Christopher's godfather."

"Why did he never marry?" Joan asked.

After another pause, Ivy said quietly, "Let's just say he's a confirmed bachelor set in his ways." There was a poignant silence interrupted by Christopher returning on his hands and knees with a gleeful Neil riding on his back. The mood was broken and they both laughed at his antics.

All in all, she was content but things began to change that summer. As usual, they were at Duncan's who was having a garden party now the weather had improved. The enclosed garden was large enough to have a gazebo erected in the centre and the patio door to the kitchen was open where a selection of canapés and open sandwiches were available. French pop music, in vogue, drifted across the lawn. It had been added to with a French theme for the day and cheeses she'd never tasted before were on display together with a good selection of wines.

For fun for most, and pretension for a few, the conversation drifted into French. Alex, for once seemed at ease and chatted amiably with Christopher; who was studying French at school, to help his linguistics. Joan was amazed at Alex's fluency and complimented him on it asking he came to be so confident in the language. For once, he was open in his reply.

"That's no great secret, my mother was from the Channel Islands and we had relatives there and in France. I spent many a happy summer there in my youth and she often spoke to me in French to help me to maintain it. That's what I'm trying to do with young Christopher here. But I've told him he can do his own homework."

"Spoilsport," said the young man. Turning to Joan, he said, *"Bonjour, Madam, ca va?"*

"Ca va tres bien, merci, Monsieur," she laughed, "and that's the limit of mine." To Alex, she said, "Do you ever go back?"

"No, the war spoilt it for me." He seemed about to say more then returned to his usual reticent self. Joan decided to leave him in peace and circulate among the other guests. She was a lot more confident now than at the first party, a word here, a joke there and a shared drink. Often she was joined by Duncan and Ivy but Ruby was noticeable by her absence. When she finally reached Bob, she remarked on this.

"Remember, Dianne," he replied, "she's suspicious of any pretty woman around Duncan." They'd talked about Dianne and the scene at Christmas after Fred had let the story out one Tuesday night. Joan had been a little surprised at first but later admitted she thought Duncan could be a bit of a rogue.

"Well, you don't have to worry about me. And do you think I'm the prettiest girl here?"

"Without doubt," and jokingly, "you've got twenty years on the others." She punched his arm. "No, really, you look stunning." It was true, in a light summer dress, high collared and fitted that suited her slim figure and showed off her legs, accentuated with white sling backs with a small heal she was the epitome of the modern sixties' woman. She was also comfortable with herself and confidence radiated from her as she meandered among the guests.

As she did so, Duncan was at her side and it looked like it was her party and she and Duncan were the hosts. As they walked together, he leaned in and whispered, "You look beautiful today, but then you always do." She didn't know what to say but decided to make light of it.

"I'll bet you say that to all the girls."

"No, only when it's true." He smiled and walked away leaving a bewildered Joan behind.

Chapter Forty-Three

Joan was confused. She genuinely liked Duncan but had not thought anything further about him. Which wasn't true in that she had entertained some fantasies about him, but fantasies, if perhaps harmful, are at least safe. She was flattered by the attention, excited by what it could mean whilst feeling guilty about Robbie. He was the first man she had ever loved and the only man she had ever slept with, but thoughts of Duncan excited her.

In the end, though, she decided that a fantasy was what it was and what it would remain. Still, her feelings swung between joy and moodiness which was not lost on Bob who wondered what he'd done. He tried everything he knew to cheer her up but to no avail. Even her mother suspected something was wrong when she phoned and came over one afternoon, taking the bus from the colliery that passed along the edge of the estate.

When she arrived, she was all business taking off her coat and, after giving Neil a cuddle, retreating into the kitchen to put the kettle on. Emerging from the kitchen with a tray she came straight to the point.

"Okay, girl, what's wrong, has something happened between you and Robbie? You're not yourself."

"No, we're fine, Robbie's busy at work most of the time and it gets a bit lonely at times." She couldn't confess to her mother the real reason why she was moody, not that she understood it herself. Her mother was unsympathetic.

"That's life, girl, as long as you and Robbie are okay, you get on with it. If you need cheering up, why don't you get changed and go into the city for a break. Don't worry about

Neil, I can have some grandma time with him. Is that all right, son," she smiled tickling him under his chin as he chuckled.

"If you're sure you don't mind, I could probably do with it." She didn't really have any desire to go into town but neither did she wish to spend the afternoon under her mother's scrutiny. "I'll just go change and go down for a couple of hours, if you don't mind."

"Take as long as you like. Just come back with a smile on your face. We'll be okay." This she said to Neil, who was now sat on her knee.

Joan went to the bedroom to change, as it was a warm day she selected a light summer dress and cardigan. Kissing Neil and telling him to behave for grandma, she said goodbye to her mother, asking again if she didn't mind then left to catch the bus from the edge of the high street.

A short while later, she got off in the market place and started to wander along the old streets window-shopping. She generally had things to buy for the house or for Neil but today, it was as if she was a teenager again, looking at the new fashions. After a while, she began to browse in the shops themselves, trying on new dresses and chatting to the salesgirls. Perhaps her mother had been right, she thought, as she started to enjoy herself, she had thought about going to the store to see the girls and see if Bob was free for lunch. But she knew that he was busy and today she wanted to be Joan again rather than Mrs Lee.

After an hour, she had bought a new dress and, with the bag in her hand, decided to treat herself to a coffee and cake at a little café she knew tucked away in a passageway, or vennel as it was known locally. She was just about to enter as she saw Duncan coming down the street with books under his arm. As he saw her, he increased his step and came up to her.

"Hello, what are you doing here, Robbie not with you?" She wasn't sure what to say, she was still nervous after the party but Duncan appeared to have forgotten about it and she wondered if she had over reacted. If anything, he seemed his usual self.

"No, he's at work. Mum's looking after Neil so I thought I'd get out for an hour. I've done a bit of shopping and I was just on my way for a coffee."

"Sounds great. I've just been to collect some books from the university Book Shop. I'm in no hurry to get back to college, there is a limit to how much tolerance one can have for callow youth. Do you mind if I join you?" She couldn't think of a reason to refuse.

"Of course not, company would be nice as long as we don't have to talk about babies and cooking. I'm domesticated out." He laughed.

"Come on then, we'll put the world to rights over scones." She followed him up the vennel and into the café where Duncan led her to a table tucked in the corner of the room. "What would you like, I can recommend the scones, I'm often in here, my college is straight opposite and I sometimes come here when I need to get off the campus for a while."

"Sounds good, but if we're having scones, I'll have tea." Duncan left to go to the small counter and returned carrying a tray.

"So what have you been buying?" She was surprised by the question, not expecting him to have any interest in her shopping.

"Nothing much, just a new dress. I don't really need it, but I was feeling a bit sorry for myself so I thought why not."

"Good for you. There's nothing wrong with thinking about yourself every now and then. So what was making you feel sorry for yourself? You always seem so happy, with Robbie and young Neil."

"I am, don't get me wrong. It's just sometimes, that I forget who I am. I have my own mind and I'm not just an accessory. You're asking about my dress, how about telling me about the books you have been buying or do you think I wouldn't understand?"

"Of course not. It's just a bit of a dry subject and I didn't think you would be interested."

"Why don't you let me be the judge of that after you tell me what they are about?" He couldn't think of an excuse not to.

"Okay, they're about British social history during the early Victorian age and specifically the industrial revolution. The emphasis is on the underlying unity of the age with a background of the new economic powers based on the development of coal and iron technology and the social and political problems arising. They also look at intellectual reactions to changing circumstances and the influence of religion and science on national life." He paused, "Sorry, I'm going into lecturer mode, I said you wouldn't be interested."

"On the contrary, I grew up in a coal mining village where they still talk about Keir Hardie. They're staunch Labour supporters, trade unionists and socialists and they might view industrialisation differently from your intellectual viewpoint."

"Don't you think it's important to look at the wider economic implications of the period, its contribution to expanding imperialism and political structure?"

"That's all well and good, but it fails to address the circumstances of the common man and how he lives."

"Not true, the church's stance, the rise of non-conformity and active trade unionism as you've pointed out are all a result." He smiled as she responded and they continued to talk until their tea had gone cold. "Well, that was interesting, tell me did you never think of going to university. You've a sharp mind."

"It was never an option. I had good grades at school but we were never encouraged to go on to higher education. A few of the girls went to teacher training college but even they were the exception and I never had any fancy for that. Besides, where I come from, you're expected to work, there's nothing more shameful than someone who doesn't pull their weight, which could be an example of the effect of your changes on national life. Besides, I never knew anybody who went to university and don't even have any idea what a college is like. I would have been a complete fish out of water."

"You have an over inflated opinion of what college is like. It's really just classrooms by any other name and a lot of students who are really not that bright. Tell you what, why don't you come with me and I'll show you the college then you can see for yourself." She looked at her watch. She realised she was curious.

"Okay, that would be interesting if it's not too much trouble."

"Come on then, and don't forget your bag!" Together, they left the café through the vennel, and across the cobbled street to the gates opposite from where the inner road dropped to the imposing Georgian front of the main college building. "Welcome to academia, not really that impressive, is it?"

"The buildings are pretty outstanding; you've become to blaze about it. You need to get out more into the industrial areas to get a better perspective."

"Ouch. You could be right though. My trouble is I went to Oxford, now that really is an impressive university."

As they walked on, a porter greeted them, "Afternoon, Dr Wright."

Joan was impressed, but keen not to show it. "Not professor then?"

"No, nothing so illustrious. I leave that to Alex. I'm merely a reader, that's something between lecturer and professor. That's me, just a little reader, I think that's what the students call me." He laughed.

"I'm sure they love you really, and all the young girls have a crush on you."

"Once upon a time perhaps, now I think they see me more as their father."

"You run yourself down, you're still an attractive man."

"Do you think so?" She blushed and looked away.

"Come on, silly, I'm only teasing." He led her through the various buildings, the main dining hall, showing her high table, past lecture halls and the college chapel. Everywhere they went, he was greeted, enthusiastically by women and she thought, with something of a snigger by the men. Finally, they came to a narrow staircase in an annex in the centre of the campus.

"What's in here?"

"This is where some of the students live and where sad people like me have offices. Come on, I'll show you." He led her up the staircase showing her the nameplates on student doors. At a landing, he opened a heavy door, "Come on welcome to my humble domain." She was expecting an office or study but was surprised to find a suite of rooms.

"This isn't what I was expecting."

"A lot of the junior lecturers live on campus. Some of us older staff keep the rooms as we need office space accessible to students and they come in handy for college functions when we decide to stay overnight. Do you want a drink, I keep sherry in here for some of my students during tutorials."

"Are they favoured students?"

"Some are, but to be honest, I sometimes need a drink with some of them." As he said this, he handed her a glass. She wandered around the room, taking in the décor and looking out of the window across the lawn.

"It must be an uncomfortable life." She said this with hardly a hint of the sarcasm she felt.

"It's a cross one has to bear." The voice came from directly behind her and she turned to find him right behind her. Before she had time to say anything, he had pulled her to him and, tilting her head, kissed her. She wanted to resist but found herself aroused and half followed, was half carried to the bedroom where they were soon thrashing on the narrow bed. All thoughts vanished from her mind as she gave herself to pleasure. It was only as they lay together later that guilt set in. *What was she doing here, what had she done?* As Duncan lay contented, tears came with great sobs that racked her body.

He looked at her shocked, "What's wrong, didn't you enjoy it?"

"Is that all it is to you, a bit of pleasure. What about my husband and son? You just got me here for this, didn't you? How long have you been planning this? Don't you think anything of Ruby?"

"You were happy to come to bed."

"Well I'm not now." Grabbing her clothes, she dressed quickly, avoiding his eyes, and snatching her bags she rushed out of the door, ignoring his protestations. He could only look on confused, he'd had many women go to his bed willingly, and a few tearful endings but never a reaction like this.

Chapter Forty-Four

Tearful, she caught the bus from the market place, paying the conductor as she avoided his eye, not wanting any sympathy or anyone asking how she was. At the edge of the high street, she took a deep breath before walking down to the house. She didn't want her mother seeing she was upset and needed time herself to come to terms with what had happened. She was under no illusions that it had been nothing but a planned seduction and the more she thought about it, she could see its pattern: his smooth introduction to her as he gave her a lift, the invite to the party and how he had callously cultivated both her and Robbie.

She also saw that she was not the first as the scene with Dianne came back to her. She didn't know what hurt most, that he had casually manipulated her with the sole intention of getting her into bed, or that she had fallen for his lies and deceit. No, she thought, what hurt the most was that she had betrayed Robbie and that he had led her to do it. The thought of Robbie tore a gasp from her and she took another deep breath.

At the door, she calmed herself before going into the hall and shouting, "Hi, Mum, I'm back, has everything been okay and has Neil behaved himself?" She forced a smile as she went into the sitting room where her mother was sat nursing a happy Neil.

"He's been no bother, have you, pet? We've had a good time this afternoon. How about you, I see you've been shopping, let's see what you've been buying?" Mustering as much enthusiasm as she could, she pulled the dress out of the bag and held it up against herself for her mother to see.

"Ooh, that's lovely, pet, and the colours perfect for you. Robbie will love you in it. Which reminds me, he rang when you were out. I told him you were shopping and I think he expected you to call in the store when you'd finished. Anyway, he said I hadn't to get the bus home and that he'd run me there in the car when he finished work. He's always been a thoughtful boy."

"Yes, I know, I don't deserve him." *Especially not now,* she thought. "Anyway, I didn't call in because I don't like disturbing him at work, I know how busy he is. Besides, when I get in with the girls, I can never get away and I needed some time to myself today." She was surprised how easily the lies came.

"Well, as long as you enjoyed yourself, and don't hassle yourself over dinner, Neil had a little nap so I took the time to make you a casserole. All you need to do is shove it the oven when you're ready. I remember how you used to like my casserole."

"Thanks, but you shouldn't have bothered."

"It's no bother, it's what mothers are for. Why don't you put on your new dress and you and Robbie have a nice night? I told him to bring a bottle of wine with him. He works too hard and you are busy with the baby. You need some time together." She felt tears coming to her eyes, he was more than she deserved and guilt hit her like a hammer.

"Thanks, Mum." Her mother put her arms around her.

"Stop that now, I just want to see you happy. Get those tears away before your husband gets home. Do you think you're the first mother who needs spoiling?" Obediently, she wiped her eyes. "That's better."

Bob arrived shortly after, picking up a gleeful Neil and pecking her on the cheek. She didn't want a peck on the cheek, she wanted him to take her in his arms and tell her everything was all right. But for that to happen, she would have to tell him everything that had happened and she couldn't do that; she didn't want to hurt him and she wasn't sure how he would react. The only thing she was certain of was that she didn't want to lose him and the more she thought this, the more she despised Duncan. Did he think he could destroy people just to get his own pleasure?

Shortly afterwards, Bob took Joan's mother home. Parting she said, "Don't forget what I've told you. Now come on young man, you can see an old lady home."

After they left, she bathed and fed Neil and put him to bed. They'd been lucky; Neil was placid child and a good sleeper. Thinking of what her mother had said, she switched the oven on before going to the bedroom to change. As she smoothed the dress down, she thought it looked nice but she didn't feel special, more that she was a fraud and a cheat. But it wasn't Robbie's fault, only hers and if Duncan had spoilt her happiness, he wasn't going to spoil his. Hands trembling, she reapplied her makeup and put on the perfume he'd bought her for Christmas.

She had just finished setting the table when she heard the car pull into the drive and was stood by it as he came into the room, "Blimey, you look gorgeous." She didn't feel gorgeous but her heart melted even as guilt consumed her.

"I'm glad you think so, you paid for this."

"You're worth every penny." He took her in his arm and kissed her. "You smell nice and so does something else. Is that your mum's casserole, she told me about it when I was driving. To be honest, I'm starving, didn't get lunch today. I know it's my fault, so don't scold me. Anyway, as per mummy's instructions, I've got a nice bottle of wine. If I'm only getting one meal today, let's make it a good one." She thought, *If anyone needs reprimanding it's me.*

"Coming up, o lord and master." She went into the kitchen to serve up as he took his jacket and tie off and took a corkscrew from the cabinet to open the wine. She'd already put glasses on the table and he poured the wine as she returned from the kitchen with their dinner. Sitting opposite each other, he raised his glass, "Cheers, my dear, now excuse a hungry man," as he attacked his dinner. She sipped her wine as she watched him.

"Robbie, do you love me?"

"Of course," he mumbled through a mouthful of food.

"Then say it please." He looked at her as he cleared his mouth.

"I love you."

"No matter what."

"Always and forever. What's brought all this on?"

"Nothing, I just like you to say it." She wanted to tell him everything, to beg his forgiveness but was too frightened of the consequences. Instead, she pecked at her food; she had deliberately given herself a small portion and more rearranged it on her plate than ate. Bob, concentrating on his own plate, failed to notice and she tidied up as soon as he'd finished. They sat after the meal drinking their wine and making small talk.

"This is nice, we should do it more often."

"Yes, we should, but I don't want food. I want you to take me to bed."

"What now, it's early."

"All the better. Please now."

She took his hand and led him up the stairs. They undressed quickly before she dragged him into the bed, clinging fiercely to him as they made love. She wanted to wipe away the memory of Duncan as quickly as she could. Bob was stunned by her ardour but was caught in the flow.

As they lay together later and she was gripping him tightly he murmured, "Remind me to send you to get a new dress more often." Before she could respond, he was asleep. As she clung to him, a tear ran down her cheek. Men could be bastards; thank heavens he was a good one. She decided she didn't deserve him but also that she would always be there for him.

Chapter Forty-Five

Bob went to the pub on Tuesday night as usual, it had become a habit since the Christmas party the previous year and he looked forward to it as a release from the constant focus on work; the other men shared his opinions, or more accurately his prejudices, and he was able to unload in a way he couldn't at work or home.

Joan had started to seem reluctant about his going but had been more relaxed about it recently. However, it was his choice and he needed it: in his mind he worked hard and took very little for himself and was entitled to some pleasure. Fred and Alex were already in the snug bar as he entered; it was their domain and now his.

He greeted them, "What, no Duncan again?" Duncan had been absent for several weeks, longer if he thought about it.

"Haven't you heard," Fred said. Fred was always the talker of the group just as Alex was always the listener. "Duncan and Ruby are moving, Ruby told Ivy there's another new development nearer the city and they're having a bungalow built there. Although knowing them, it won't be a small one."

"What's brought all that on, I thought they were settled here?" Fred looked at Alex who said nothing.

"Who knows, Duncan has always been a party animal but Ruby prefers the quiet life. It's also better for both of them for work. And we're not getting any younger, we're not youngsters like you and Joan. How is she by the way?" Bob had been waiting for the question.

"Putting on weight." When the other two looked at him askance he laughed and added, "She's pregnant and I'm going to be a father again."

"Congratulations, old boy." This from Alex. "It calls for a little celebration, I'll get some drinks in."

"It's my shout," protested Bob.

"Not this time." Alex went to the bar and returned not only with three pints but also three whiskeys. It was the first of many as word spread out across the pub and their friends brought over more drinks. Eventually, Alex asked, "How is Joan doing?" In typical fashion, it had all been about a celebration, about the proud father and not the poor girl who would carry the child and go through labour.

"To be honest, she's a bit moody. She was fine when she was expecting Neil but this time I'm tiptoeing around her a bit. Let's just say, she's a bit snappy at the moment. With Neil, everything was planned, but this time, it's come as a bit of a surprise. Maybe that's the difference?"

"Could be, but they say no two pregnancies are the same. That could be it. But then again what would I know about it."

"Some men are born bachelors," cut in Fred, "and Alex is one of them. Isn't that right, Alex?"

"You could be right," answered Alex quietly. Then, looking at Bob added, "Come on, one for the road and then we'd better get this boy home while he can still stand or his waspish wife will have words for us."

One drink later, they took their leave, Alex and Fred on either side of Bob as they weaved the short way back to his home. At the end of the drive, they said goodbye and watched as he reached the door and let himself in. Joan was coming down the stairs as he came through the door.

"You're back, I was just starting to get worried." As he staggered, "How much have you had to drink?"

"It's not my fault, I told the guys you were expecting and they kept buying me drinks."

"And forcing you to drink them I take it." Her look was withering. "And who was there."

"The usual crowd apart from Duncan," he paused as he remembered something, "he hasn't been there for weeks, longer as I come to think of it. But apparently, Fred said he and Ruby are moving. There having some fancy place built nearer the city. A bungalow by all accounts. Fred was joking that they're all getting older. I didn't think Duncan looked that old. What do you think?"

"He's dapper, but yes, he's starting to look his age." The last with some bitterness.

"I always thought you liked him."

"Well, you thought wrong."

"Well, I'll miss him."

Under her breath, she said as she walked away, "Well, I won't."

Chapter Forty-Six

Joan was having a miserable pregnancy. With Neil, she'd been looking forward to his arrival, getting his room and clothes together but now she found every task a chore. She didn't really want the child, not for herself but because she wasn't sure whose baby it was. She hoped in her heart that it was Robbie's but was frightened in case it wasn't. Bob couldn't understand her mood.

He put it down to depression and asked if she wanted to see the doctor but she refused; she knew she wasn't depressed, angry, guilt ridden and trapped yes, but depressed no. She began to put an act on for Bob's sake, he deserved better than her misery. Oblivious he thought she was recovering but accepted that she was feeling delicate and was solicitous in his time at home. His attentions only made her guilt more intense and led to her getting snappy with him. She could see she was hurting him but couldn't find a way of dealing with it.

Things changed in the early spring when she went into labour. It started in the evening and Bob, after numerous calls to the hospital, and timings of contractions, finally bundled her in the car and drove down to the hospital. He was on hand all the time she was in the delivery room and walking anxiously outside as the contractions quickened and the pain increased until she was at last crying out.

Fortunately, it was a quick delivery, short but sharp. The fussing midwifes announced she had a beautiful little girl and after she had been buddled up, placed her in her arms. As they did so, everything changed as she gazed at the little face and the child opened her eyes, looked at her, smiled and went to sleep. Love comes in many ways but when it hits the effect is always the same, all-consuming and eternal.

As she looked, she whispered, "Hello, little one, I'm sorry for everything but it wasn't your fault and you are not going to suffer, and nor is your dad."

Bob was brought into the delivery room to meet the infant. As he gazed down, he too felt a tug on his heart, "She's beautiful, just like her mum. You've done well, girl."

"No, we've done well, and you're right, she is beautiful. We're a proper family now and that is how it's going to be. Just you, me, Neil and Gillian." She saw his puzzled look, "Don't ask, the name just came to me and it seemed right."

"It's more than right, it's perfect." Just then he was interrupted by the midwife.

"Come on now, young man, time to go and let us get on with our work. We have things to do and your wife is tired and needs some rest. You can come back at visiting time. Now, say goodbye to your wife and daughter and say you'll see them later." Bob obediently kissed Joan and planted a light one on Gillian's brow. After he had gone, Joan made a silent promise, Bob was a good man and she did love him, and she loved the new baby for herself. They were going to be a family she would see to that.

Joan was as good as her word, Neil and Gillian came first then Bob. Everything at home was kept perfect, spotless, with Bob and the children turned out immaculately. She doted on the children, always there, dropping them off and picking them up from school, and as they got older, being in when they returned. She was active on the PTA and sweated over their homework with them encouraging them to work hard and strive for what they wanted. Bob also encouraged them, improvement was what had driven him all his life and he genuinely wanted the best for his children, but Joan interceded and softened his approach when he was getting too stern.

As much as she loved, Neil she doted on Gillian, if dad was the authority she was the best friend. They shared everything, going shopping together, Joan wiping her tears when she spilt with her first boyfriend and visiting her when she went away to college. When she graduated from what was one of the finest universities in the world, she watched proudly with tears running down her cheeks. Nothing ever could, or did, change the absolute love she felt for her daughter. But things inevitably changed.

The change came when, after graduation, Gillian moved to London to work. She still came home occasionally when holidays allowed, but it wasn't the same as college vacations when the visits were endless. As her own life developed and the visits became more protracted, Joan discovered a hole in her life. She missed the endless chatter of a house full of children: Neil, as the eldest, had left home earlier and was also in London but it was Gillian whose loss she felt the keenness.

She'd dedicated her life to her children, and when they'd left, with her blessing, to pursue their careers, the centre of her world collapsed. Bob and her still functioned as a couple but had grown apart as she'd doted on the children, following their own lives. She retreated into herself, having few interests outside of the children. She felt envious of other women whose daughters still lived close, visiting regularly and providing grandchildren. But she never wanted her daughter trapped into a life she didn't want just for her sake.

But there were other consequences of her loneliness, always smart she lost pride in her appearance and, without her daughter to nag her, started to let herself go. She wasn't dirty, she could never be that, but clothes no longer held any interest for her and she and Bob ceased going out together. When her work in the house was done, she slumped in front of the TV, living through the endless soaps. Bob busied himself with work on the house, the only thing that didn't change was his nights with Fred and Alex, every Tuesday and Thursday night and Sunday afternoons in winter.

Chapter Forty-Seven

Joan walked with Bob through the college gates on the day of Duncan's funeral. The man had died as he'd lived, holding Ruby's hand as he watched the nurses out of the corner of his eye.

Duncan was not a religious man but his long service at the university and his standing in the college meant the service would be conducted in the college chapel before cremation. The only stipulation Duncan had ever made, on the rare occasions he and Ruby had discussed such matters, was that he didn't wish to be interred in the cold earth; he'd seen to many lonely graves of his comrades during the war and the thought still filled him with dread.

"The chapels this way," Joan said to Bob as she steered him to the left as they passed the gates.

"How do you know that?" She quickly recovered; she couldn't tell him that was how she remembered it. She was surprised at how the events of that day were so clearly etched in her mind. She'd buried them so deeply but now they were rearing up again. But she couldn't tell him that.

"Because I can see the stained glass at the top of the windows." To change the subject, "Come on, let's take seats." Fred and Alex were stood inside by the door and greeted them as they came through.

"Hello, Bob, good of you to come, and Joan. It's been a while, how you keeping?"

"Very well," she lied. To Fred she added, "How's Ivy by the way?"

"She's well. She's with Ruby, she's the nearest thing she has to family, Ruby has none and they never could have children so she's on her own unhappily."

"I often wondered why they never had children. I always thought it was because Ruby was a career woman, not that she couldn't."

"You've got it wrong," cut in Alex, "Ruby was okay, it was Duncan who couldn't, they wanted children earlier and went through all the tests and that's when it came out. In truth, I don't think Ruby was ever that maternal but she thought it might settle Duncan down. It's probably for the best, I think Duncan would have made a lousy father. I feel sorry for Ruby now though, she's all alone, apart from us."

"Wasn't he bothered?" she asked.

"Not in the slightest. Most men would feel incomplete but Duncan merely took it to mean that he could carry on with no risk of recriminations. Not that it had ever stopped him before." Joan felt that she had been punched and caught Alex looking at her out of the corner of his eye. She always felt that he saw more than he should and quickly looked away.

To break the ice, she said to Bob, "We'd better take our seats." As they walked down the aisle, she noticed that the congregation appeared to have a disproportionate number of women in it, or was that just her imagination. As they took the seats, there was a signal from the rear and the coffin was born in with Ruby, clinging on to Ivy's arm walking behind it.

Alex and Fred followed them and took seats at the front as it was placed by the altar. Joan was shocked at Ruby's appearance: she'd always been so smart, prim and proper even, and handsome despite her formidable demeanour. Now she was a shell of her former self, frail and worn.

The service began with the chaplain greeting the congregation and saying a few words about Dr Wright and his service to the college before reading from the gospel of St John 14 of the many rooms in my father's house. As he finished, he announced that Dr Wright's oldest friend, Professor McIntyre, would like to say a few words.

Alex got up from his seat and went to the lectern. Clearing his throat, he looked at the people gathered, "First of all, thank you for all coming, I'm sure Duncan would have appreciated it. We all thought we knew him but he was a complex man. Everybody remembers the party animal that Duncan was, the

221

best host and the life and soul of any event. But let's not forget the gifted academic he was. It may surprise you to know what a quiet student he was in his younger days. I first met him at Oxford before the war when we were both undergraduates. Believe it or not I was the boisterous one then and Duncan the quiet, committed academic," this raised a few smiles from the younger members of the college. "I think that then he was like a lot of us students, slightly arrogant but looking for love." This raised even more smiles. "But the war changed all that, in fact it changed all of us. What you won't know is that Duncan; Captain Wright, had an illustrious war record, but saw things that scarred him. He was badly wounded in Italy; that limp wasn't for effect, but had the good fortune to meet a young female officer who helped him to recover both physically and mentally. She did such a good job that he recovered and married her and they've been together ever since. I met Duncan again after my own service and we've been firm friends ever since. I'll miss him and cannot express how I feel about his loss so if you don't mind I'll quote a poem that sums it up better than I can." He paused then began:

The moment that you died,
my heart was torn in two,
one side filled with heartache,
the other died with you.
I often lie awake at night,
when the world is fast asleep, and
take a walk down memory lane,
with tears upon my cheeks.
Remembering you is easy,
I do it every day,
but missing you is heartache
that never goes away.
I hold you tightly within my heart
and there you will remain.
Until the joyous day arrives
that we will meet again.'

He finished to silence. The final hymn was sung as the coffin was carried out with the friends following. Bob looked at Joan, "What do you want to do?" he asked.

"Take me home," she replied.

Chapter Forty-Eight

Three months later and another funeral saw Bob and Joan walking under an umbrella to the crematorium. It was a miserable day, overcast and drizzling; not even proper rain, just enough to justify raincoats and ensure misery. In many ways, it matched the event as they gathered for Ruby's cremation. She'd never recovered from Duncan's death and had slowly wasted away with only Ivy visiting her. It was Ivy who'd arranged for her to go into care and finally into a hospice where she had passed away, alone and lonely.

Ivy had arranged the funeral; Ruby had been adamant she didn't wish a church service. She'd gone along with Duncan's because of his attachment to the college and their desire to honour him. But she had a lifelong distaste for the church, and particularly the clergy, and had insisted on a non-religious send off. There were few people in attendance, a small official contingent from the civil service, an equally small number of old work colleagues and of course the old friends Alex, Ivy and Fred. Bob had felt obliged to go and was surprised when Joan had offered to go with him but was grateful for the company. He was also happy with the change that had come over Joan recently.

Joan had changed following Duncan's funeral. The revelation that he could not have children had hit her like a punch in the stomach. But later, it had been a relief and the shadow that had hung over her for years had been blown away. The lie that she had been carrying for years no longer had substance; she knew she had let Bob down but now saw that she had been a victim who'd been abused and it had spoilt enough of her life and Bob's. It hadn't happened overnight but quickly enough, she taken and interest in her appearance again, losing weight and dressing carefully. TV soaps had been consigned to history and she'd started talking to Bob again.

The service was over quickly; Alex again spoke a few words and a representative from the civil service gave a short speech about her contribution to government and how she was respected and then it was time for the curtains to close across the coffin. They trooped quietly from the hall and gathered outside. Alex was waiting.

"Hello, its good of you to come, there's tea and refreshments across at the golf club. Please come." Bob looked at Joan.

"We will, of course," she answered for them.

"Excellent, I'll see you there then." As he turned, they crossed to the car and drove the short distance to the golf club opposite. Bob was surprised at Joan's response.

"I thought you didn't like Ruby."

"I didn't years ago, but I see things differently now. You men may have thought Duncan was a great guy but I think he caused Ruby a lot of heartache. She must have really loved him to put up with it. I feel sorry for her and it's no hardship to show some respect."

They pulled up outside the club and walked into the lounge where the sparse guests were stood in uncomfortable small groups. They helped themselves to tea and stood to one side. Ivy approached them as they observed the other guests.

"Hello, it's good of you to come. And you, Joan, we haven't spoken for too long. Ruby would have been happy that you've come. So am I, I've got a surprise for you." She turned and signalled to a younger couple who came over. "You must remember my son Christopher, and this is his wife, Emma. He's a bit of an academic like Alex but he's an English lecturer."

Joan looked at the man who was tall and elegant unlike his father who was short and stocky. He must take after his mother's side she thought although he reminded her of Alex. Most startlingly was that his wife strongly resembled her younger self. "Of course, I remember him, my dancing partner of old." She saw him blush.

"It's good to see you again. I have many happy memories of those times. Aunt Ruby was different then too. You know she left all her money to me?"

"I didn't, but she was always fond of you." They chatted for a while until she turned to Bob, "It's time we were going." They left the hall and got back in the car.

"What do you want to do now, ready for home?"

"No, Robbie Lee, we're in the car and you can take me out for lunch. You used to be good at finding places to go to try to impress me and I could use a proper drink. And that doesn't mean posh fish and chips and certainly not Babycham. Although I doubt they sell it anymore, thankfully." He smiled.

"At your service, madam. I'll see what I can do."